Lions
An Imprint of HarperCollinsPublishers

CLASS TRIP

There were seven of us when we started out.

Someone - I think it was James - said that seven was a magic number. That magicians - real magicians like Merlin, the wizard, not the ones who pull rabbits out of hats - had always believed it was a powerful number. One that protected from harm.

Hah. Some magic.

But then, we didn't stay seven long. One by one the group grew smaller. And finally there were only two of us.

Two is not a magical number. When one of the two is a murderer.

More heart-stopping Nightmares...

NIGHTMARES

CLASS TRIP

Bebe Faas Rice

Lions

An Imprint of HarperCollinsPublishers

First published in the USA in 1993 by
HarperCollins Publishers Inc.
First published in Great Britain in Lions in 1993
1 3 5 7 9 10 8 6 4 2

Lions is an imprint of HarperCollins Children's Books,
a division of HarperCollins Publishers Ltd, 77-85 Fulham
Palace Road, Hammersmith, London W6 8JB

Text copyright © 1993 by Bebe Faas Rice
and Daniel Weiss Associates, Inc.

ISBN 0 00 674700 0

The author asserts the moral right to be identified as the
author of the work.

Printed and bound in Great Britain
by HarperCollins Book Manufacturing Ltd, Glasgow

In loving memory of Miss Anne G. Wilson, principal of Garfield Elementary School, Ottumwa, Iowa, who always told me I would be a writer of books someday.

ONE

In the end . . .

So this was it. This was how it was supposed to end. The way it had been planned right from the start. The two of us, killer and victim. Final victim. Victim number six.

For a brief moment we said nothing. We simply stared into each other's eyes. What were we looking for? A reprieve from death? An explanation? Forgiveness?

But what can a victim say to change a murderer's mind? What argument is strong enough to stop a killing machine?

And why should a murderer try to explain why it was necessary to kill five—soon to be six—people? For forgiveness?

Do you need forgiveness when you've

1

committed the perfect crime, or is that only for those who will get caught?

This murderer would not get caught. . . .

There were seven of us when we started out.

Someone—I think it was James—said that seven was a magic number. That magicians—real magicians like Merlin, the wizard, not the ones who pull rabbits out of hats—had always believed it was a powerful number. One that protected from harm.

Hah. Some magic.

But then, we didn't stay seven long. One by one the group grew smaller. And finally there were only two of us.

Two is not a magical number. When one of the two is a murderer.

But in the beginning there were seven. Six were long-standing members of the elite "in" group of Oakbridge High. True aristocrats, as high-school royalty goes.

And then there was me.

I was the newcomer. The one who wanted to be a part of the inner circle. To sit at the special table in the school cafeteria. To be envied because I ran around with the football heroes and *the best-looking and most popular girls on campus.*

And so I was one of the seven, the special, selected seven, that made the trip to Shadow Island.

I paid a high price to become one of that group. I would live to regret it. But at the time, I thought it was a price well worth paying.

I was wrong.

I was dead wrong.

TWO

"What a dump!" Christabel said, standing in the doorway of the youth hostel.

She struck a pose, one hand on her hip and the other waving an imaginary cigarette. "What an unbelievable dump!"

She was doing her Bette Davis routine. I'd seen it many times. It wasn't all that good, but who was I to criticize the queen of Oakbridge High?

Every high school must have its reigning beauty, just as every wolf pack needs a leader. And that's what Christabel Collins was. Queen. Leader. Golden-haired goddess. She ruled the best, the most exclusive clique in school. The one everyone wanted to be a part of, but which included only the prettiest, most popular girls, like Christabel and Melanie Downes and Tracy Fisher.

And me. I was in the group now. Lucky me.

Are you proud of me now, Michael? I'm doing it only for you. You always used to say that living well was the best revenge. I miss you, Michael.

Melanie Downes pushed me aside in her eagerness to follow Christabel into the lounge of the hostel. She always seemed to hang on to Christabel's coattails. Maybe she figured some of Christabel's glitter would rub off on her if she stood close enough.

"I don't think it's all that bad, Chris," she said. "After all, we're only going to be here one night before we leave for Shadow Island."

The hostel was a two-story wooden building. It was unpainted, both inside and out, and the boards had turned a silvery gray with age. It was built in a simple rectangular shape, like an old army barracks, and looked as if it had been here, at the head of the Doone River, for a long, long time.

A small private college owned the hostel and rented it out to school groups and hiking and canoeing clubs. From the looks of things, we were the first—and only—group to stay there

6

this season. I could see a thick layer of dust on the stairs leading to the top floor, and some of last fall's leaves that had blown in from the porch still littered the foyer, in front of the check-in desk.

No clerk or receptionist manned the desk. A large sign, propped against the wall, told us where to find the caretaker and urged us to leave the building as clean as we found it.

That won't be hard, I thought. Even my room at home is cleaner than this.

Christabel was right. It really *was* a dump.

In the lounge Melanie plunked her cosmetic case down on a vinyl-upholstered chair that had a large rip on the seat. I could hear makeup bottles rattle and clink.

Naturally Melanie *would* have to bring a bag full of cosmetics on a week-long trip into the wilds! Heaven forbid she be caught without her frosted-blue eye shadow.

Melanie was as gorgeous in a brunette, dark-eyed way as Christabel was stunningly blond. You had to be good-looking to run in this crowd. I know. It took a major make-over—hair, wardrobe, body, contact lenses—for me to make the grade.

But for all her looks and charm, there was a

7

streak of bitchiness in Melanie that lay, only barely submerged, just beneath the surface.

Somewhere, somehow, I'd offended her. Maybe it was because my father owns a successful chain of pharmacies, which makes my family reasonably wealthy, unlike hers. Or maybe because, although I was basically a "science nerd," I'd managed to crack the inner sanctum, the holy of holies, the "in" group.

I always had to be on my guard against Melanie. That girl must have lain awake nights thinking up ways to dump on me. And the worst part of it was, she always caught me by surprise. I'd promise myself the next time she said something bitchy, I'd be waiting for her with the perfect reply—something really cool. Something that would make her sorry she ever tried to mess with me. But I could never win. She'd let me have it, and while I was trying to figure out a perfect comeback, she'd give me that smug smile of hers, and I'd know she'd beat me again.

There were heavy footsteps on the porch, and Ron Johnson staggered through the door, loaded down with a bulging backpack and a huge ice chest containing some of the perishable food we would be needing for our week of roughing it on the island.

It was a heavy load, but Ron had the muscles to carry it.

Over six feet tall and ruggedly handsome, Ron was, without question, the most popular boy at Oakbridge High. He was the captain of the football team, president of the student government, and involved in at least three other clubs. All those assets, of course, made him the perfect partner for Christabel Collins.

I didn't think Christabel was as crazy about Ron as he was about her. Christabel was a junior, as I was, but Ron would be graduating in June. I asked her once what she would do next year with him off at college. Would she miss him terribly?

She had only laughed. "I'm sure I'll find someone to help me pass the lonely hours, Angie," she'd said. "You know that old saying— men are like streetcars. If you miss one, another will be coming along right behind."

"Where do you want all this stuff, Christabel?" Ron asked. "We'll be loading it in the canoes tomorrow morning."

"Mr. and Mrs. Holmberg haven't gotten here

yet," she told him. "Let's just pile everything in the middle of the room and sort it out later."

"Are you sure we brought enough food?" Tracy Fisher asked. Tracy was a tall, sandy-haired jockette. Although she ate like Jaws, the great white shark, she never gained an ounce. There wasn't much meat on her bones, but what was there was artistically arranged.

Tracy was one of the more likable members of the group that was heading for Shadow Island. She hadn't made any efforts to get into Christabel's clique. Just the opposite; she couldn't have cared less. Tracy was pretty, athletic, and headed for Stanford University when she graduated next year, financially backed by a generous swimming scholarship. She didn't need to be a member of the in group in order to feel good about herself.

"We have more than enough," Melanie told her. "Unless Angie"—she looked at me slyly from beneath her thick eyelashes—"goes on one of her eating binges."

I'm thinner now than I used to be. I was never really fat, but I did trim down some recently. I didn't realize Melanie had ever noticed me before I started hanging out with Christabel. I guess she had, and now she obviously was not about to let me forget my chubbier days.

I glared at her, and she smiled. When would I learn to smarten up and ignore her when she yanked my chain?

"Where are James and Chip?" Christabel asked.

"They're locking up the cars and bringing in the rest of the gear," replied Ron. "You know James. That guy's such a worrier! I told him we could leave some of the stuff out there overnight, but he's nervous about someone sneaking around in the dead of night and ripping us off."

"Well, we all know James has problems with his nerves," Melanie said.

"What do you mean?" I asked.

Christabel and Melanie exchanged glances.

"Don't tell me you believed him when he said he went off for a couple of weeks last fall because his grandmother was sick and they thought she was going to die!" Christabel said incredulously. "Honestly, Angie, I thought you were smarter than that."

"You mean that's not why he was gone?"

"Of course not. His grandmother's as healthy as a horse."

"So where did he go?"

11

"Are you serious?" Christabel asked. "You mean you really don't know?"

"No. I mean yes, I'm serious. No, I don't know."

"He'd been real depressed for weeks. You must have noticed."

"I really didn't know James very well then, Christabel. We only had one class together."

And I wasn't noticing much those awful days last fall. That was when Michael . . . died. Michael, my first, my best, my only friend. We'd just discovered we were more than friends, that we loved each other when . . . when it happened.

"Well, trust me, Angie," Christabel was saying. "He'd gotten himself into this awful depression where he just kind of moped around all the time. Finally his parents took him away to a hospital, where they gave him pills and treatments and stuff. He's pretty much okay now."

"We hope," Melanie said with a nasty laugh.

"But what was his problem?" I asked. "What was he depressed about?"

Christabel suddenly became very busy sorting through the gear Ron had piled up in the middle of the room.

"How should I know? That's his business, Angie, not mine."

Christabel was hiding something. Something about James. Knowing Christabel and her self-centered attitude toward other people's feelings, it was obvious she had been mixed up somehow in James's emotional breakdown. If she hadn't been, she would have had no problem airing James's dirty laundry.

Chip Marshall stuck his head through the door and called out, "Hey, everybody. If you're fooling around or smoking old banana peels, you'd better cut it out. The Holmbergs' van is coming up the drive."

We'd come in two cars—Christabel and Ron, Melanie and Chip in one, and Tracy, James, and I in the other.

Chip was Melanie's boyfriend. He was athletic and popular, but not particularly smart. He couldn't be, considering the fact he thought he was Mr. Lucky himself, the king of the hill, to be sweet, sexy little Melanie's main man. I rest my case.

"What I don't do for love," Chip said, with a mock leer in Melanie's direction. "Imagine, a whole week in Mr. Holmberg's company."

"Come off it, Chip," Tracy said. "We all know

why you've come on this trip. You're hoping to get Melanie alone out in the deep, dark woods."

"That's not a bad idea," Chip said. "It ought to increase my knowledge of biology. You know, the birds and the bees and all that stuff."

Melanie sniffed indignantly, but I could tell she was pleased. Chip might never become a rocket scientist, but he was a hunk, and there were dozens of girls at Oakbridge High just itching to get their hands on him.

"What happened to James?" I asked Chip. "Don't tell me he's going to stand guard over the cars all night!"

Chip rolled his eyes at me and waggled a finger in my direction.

"Aha! Just as I suspected, Angie," he joked. "You're starting to get the hots for James. Poor guy, he doesn't stand a chance now."

"Cut it out, Chip," I said. "Just because I asked a simple question, it doesn't mean I . . . that James and I are . . ."

"Of course not, Angie darling," Melanie put in silkily. "We all know perfectly well that you *aren't* or *haven't* with any guy, much less James Sherwood."

I thought of Michael, and how close we'd

been. Melanie, in spite of all her bragging, would never know anything like that.

If it's true that time heals all wounds, why do I still feel this terrible pain when I remember Michael?

I drifted over to the grimy picture window and looked out.

James was on the top steps of the porch, talking animatedly with the Holmbergs. I knew why James had come on this trip. He was eager to get some extra academic credits to make up for the time he'd lost by his absence last fall.

Mr. Holmberg was head of the science department at Oakbridge. Every spring break he took a small group of students on a camp-out to an island in a remote part of the state. The purpose of the expedition was to study the flora and fauna of the heavily wooded island, and Mr. Holmberg was always generous in giving extra science credits to those making the trip with him. A week on Shadow Island and a decent written report were enough to ensure a minimum grade of B– in science.

The reason the girls—Christabel, Melanie, and Tracy—had come on the trip was the same as James's. Grades. And they had begged me to come with them—well, Christabel and Tracy had begged me—because science is my strongest subject, and they thought I could help them on the island with the research and later with their reports.

"Please come, Angie," Christabel had urged. "I definitely have to go on this thing. My parents will simply kill me if I screw up my grades and don't get accepted by any of the really *good* colleges."

"Please, Angie," Tracy had added. "All that swimming practice this semester hasn't left much time for homework. I might lose my swimming scholarship if I don't maintain a high grade average. I can really use this extra credit."

Ron and Chip's reasons for coming were obvious.

First, there was the excuse to be with Christabel and Melanie day and night. The night part really seemed to intrigue them. And second, it sounded like their kind of fun. Canoeing down the river. Grubbing around in the woods. Not having to shave, or even bathe. It was their idea of a real he-man holiday.

The trip, as explained to us earlier by Mr. Holmberg, would begin with a long canoe ride down the Doone River, then onto the smaller, narrower, Blye River, which, in turn, would empty into Storm Lake, a dark, cliff-rimmed lake in a sparsely settled western corner of Vermont.

"Shadow Island is situated directly in the center of the lake," Mr. Holmberg had informed us. "It is so named because the high cliffs that surround the lake cast shadows—beginning in the early afternoon—over the island."

A senior girl, Cindy Morris, who'd been on the trip the year before, told us, "The island's pretty bleak. Spooky, even. There's an old abandoned cabin there that you'll be staying in. It used to be a hunting lodge, but that was ages ago. You'll be roughing it, all right. Believe me, you'll earn every credit Mr. Holmberg gives you!"

And so here we were, at the jumping-off point for the trip: a hostel at the head of the Doone River, where we'd spend the night before we started out early the next morning.

Cindy had warned us we'd be roughing it.

It was rough, all right.

It was a killer.

THREE

That night we all drove to the nearest town for pizza. I knew we would. Christabel was practically a pizza junkie, and the others always did what Christabel wanted. Naturally.

The Holmbergs stayed behind at the hostel.

"Don't you worry about us, now," Mrs. Holmberg had said in her fussy, prissy voice. "You go out and enjoy those pizzas. You'll be eating nothing but camp cooking all next week."

Mrs. Holmberg's father, someone told me, had been a headmaster in an old-fashioned English-style prep school. Some of the school's formality must have rubbed off on Mrs. Holmberg. She wasn't much older than my mother, actually, but she seemed positively ancient. Her weird, old-fashioned ways were the joke of

Oakbridge High, although privately I thought she was pretty nice.

Mrs. Holmberg was a frail, thin little woman in contrast to her husband, an outdoorsy, barrel-chested man. It was rumored he spent his weekends hiking nature trails, binoculars in hand, in search of some rarely sighted bird. Ron said he saw him once in a park with a butterfly net, running after a choice specimen. He said Mr. Holmberg looked exactly like one of those dancing elephants in the Disney movie *Fantasia*.

I wandered into the kitchen while Christabel and Melanie were primping for their hot night on the town.

The kitchen, like the rest of the hostel, was cold and barren. Mrs. Holmberg was standing at the stove, heating milk for what she called her "Happy Hour" cocoa.

The Holmbergs were famous for their predinner cocoa. Mrs. Holmberg taught home ec and was always giving us lectures on her ideas of right living—like avoiding alcohol and watching out for tea and coffee and not eating fatty, sugary things.

"And so," she always concluded, "no alcoholic Happy Hours for us. We have high-fiber bran wafers and artificially sweetened cocoa instead. Very relaxing, and it removes that terrible urge to *stuff* at supper."

Mr. Holmberg must be a closet stuffer, I often thought. Something—and it sure wasn't high-fiber bran wafers—was giving him a real Santa Claus waist.

Mrs. Holmberg looked up and smiled as I joined her at the rusty antique stove. I peered down at the milk, which was just coming to a boil.

"May I do something, Mrs. Holmberg?" I asked. "I'm just hanging around, waiting for everyone else to get ready."

"Why thank you, dear," Mrs. Holmberg said brightly. "How nice to see good manners in a young person these days. If you'll finish making the cocoa for me, I'll get out the bran wafers."

Bran wafers. Some Happy Hour.

"I do hope, dear, you realize that living conditions on Shadow Island are, well, quite primitive," she said, her back to me as she set the wafers on a plate. She'd even brought paper doilies with her. "But, as they say, *c'est la vie*. I'm married to a dedicated scientist, so I'm prepared to sacrifice comfort for the pursuit of knowledge. I hope you will be similarly motivated this coming week."

I promised her I would and managed to give her the impression that nothing—I mean *nothing*—was too much to suffer for the sake of my education.

When we left for the pizza parlor, the Holmbergs were sitting before a roaring fire in the lounge, sipping their cocoa. They looked cozy and contented.

I sat next to James at the Pizza Oven.

I'd known him slightly back in the days when I was a "science nerd," with my thick glasses, floppy, unflattering clothes, pocket protector, and membership in the Science Honor Society.

He'd been nice to me then, even though I'd been a campus nobody at the time, and I liked him for it.

James was good-looking, but not in the big-jock style of Chip and Ron. James's face was thin, finely boned, and sensitive. Although he had muscles in all the right places, he was slender and wiry, with a narrow waist that made his broad shoulders seem even broader.

James had grown up with Ron and Chip, and the boys seemed to respect him for his intelligence and common sense. He didn't act as though he had a swollen head because he moved in the highest circles of Oakbridge High. Just the opposite. He seemed almost a little embarrassed about it. I'd recognized that back in those days when I was a social nothing.

The booths in the Pizza Oven were rickety and horseshoe-shaped. We were packed in knee to knee.

James's thigh was pressed against mine. He wasn't doing it deliberately. There was nothing intimate about it. So why was I so aware of the warmth of his body, and why did I feel all silly and romantic about it?

No, I reminded myself, I mustn't get involved with James. Not now. It wouldn't be loyal to my memories of Michael.

"Look at that guy over there, Christabel," Melanie said, a string of cheese trailing from her mouth to a slice of pizza. "Doesn't he remind you a little of that geek who had a crush on you last fall?"

We all looked.

A boy our age was sitting at a table by the door. He was dark-haired and wore granny glasses.

"Yeah. Kind of," Christabel said. "What was his name? I can't remember."

"I think it was Michael," Melanie said.

"Michael Giddings?" I asked. My voice was clear and steady, but under the table, my fists were clenched. "Are you talking about Michael Giddings?"

"Yeah, that was his name. You knew him?" Christabel sounded surprised. I think she forgot sometimes that I hadn't always hung out with her.

"Yes," I said. "I knew him. He was my friend."

And he did not have a crush on Christabel. Not really. I was the one he loved. He just admired her looks a little, that's all. Doesn't everyone?

"Well, of course he was your friend, Angie," Melanie drawled. "Maybe the others don't remember you in your previous incarnation as a proper little bookworm, but I do. And I'll just bet you were the friend and defender of every geek and creepazoid at Oakbridge High."

She made it sound like an insult. Anyone who was friendly to what she called a "geek" was a real loser to Melanie.

"Michael wasn't a geek," I said quickly. "He

24

was smart, something you'll never understand, Melanie."

Melanie smiled. I hated that smile. It was so smug and superior.

"That's right," she said. "Smart enough to drive off a cliff one night when he'd been drinking like a fish. Brilliant. Just brilliant."

Oh Michael. What a waste. Why did you do it, Michael?

"I'm another one who remembers Angie when she was a 'proper little bookworm,'" James put in. He was trying to smooth over what was turning into an awkward situation, with me glaring at Melanie and her smiling like a malicious Mona Lisa. "And I thought she looked pretty cute in that ponytail and those horn-rimmed glasses. By the way, what'd you do with those horn-rims, Angie? I kind of miss them."

I flashed James a grateful smile. "They're in my bureau drawer. I wear contacts now."

Melanie started to open her mouth, but James hastily cut her off.

"So—" he asked. "What time are we supposed to leave tomorrow?"

"I'm not leaving before the sun comes up,"

Christabel said. "I'm definitely *not* a morning person."

Ron put his arm around her and drew her to him. "No, you're definitely at your best at night, Christabel. And I'm real glad you are."

Christabel blushed, not because she was particularly modest, but because she had that clear, almost translucent type of skin that showed every emotion. She was probably remembering what they'd been doing the night before up at Lookout Point.

Ron gave her a knowing smile before he turned to James and said, "I think we should leave around eight tomorrow morning. That ought to be early enough. Right after breakfast."

"I hope you don't expect us girls to do the cooking like faithful little squaws. This is an equal-opportunity trip, you know." Christabel pouted prettily. Ron bent forward and kissed her on the tip of her little upturned nose.

"Coffee and juice is enough for me," Chip said. "I'll make the coffee if Melanie will keep me company in the kitchen."

He gazed at her, moony-eyed. I couldn't figure out how any guy—even Chip, who was hardly a student of human nature—could be fooled by someone like Melanie. Which just goes to show you that life is definitely *not* fair.

"I think we brought cold cereal," I said before he made an even bigger fool of himself than he usually did around Melanie. "And fruit. Oh, and yogurt. That's a pretty good breakfast, don't you think?"

"Trust you, Angie, to have the food situation all figured out," Melanie said with a musical laugh. "Personally, I couldn't care less. I never eat breakfast."

Was she never going to stop needling me because, once upon a time, I'd been a hearty eater?

"Then I sure hope you're not in my canoe," I said. "I'm not doing your share of paddling because you're weak with hunger. If you've got to diet, do it another time."

That hit her where it really hurt. Melanie was always on a diet.

Tracy snickered. She was sitting on the other side of James and had been pretty quiet up until now. Tracy never said much, but when she did, it was always something sensible.

"Don't worry, Angie," she said. "I've worked out the travel arrangements, and Melanie won't be in your canoe."

27

She turned to James and continued, "Since Angie and I came in your car, James, I figured we'd probably go in your canoe, too. The three of us make a pretty good team. Ron and Christabel can go in the second canoe. They'll be carrying most of the food with them, since Ron is the strongest and most experienced canoeist. Chip and Melanie can travel together, and the Holmbergs will be out front, leading the way, in their own canoe."

"Great!" Chip agreed enthusiastically. "And when we get to the island, I hope you guys will give Melanie and me a little space, know what I mean?"

Tracy and James exchanged an amused glance.

Lately I'd begun to suspect that Tracy had a secret crush on James. He didn't seem to return the interest, though. Maybe he didn't realize how she felt about him. James treated Tracy the way he did everyone else—friendly, like a pal. A lot of girls assumed he was flirting with them, but he wasn't. That's just the way he was. Friendly.

"I've got this theory about James," Christabel had told me recently. "He's one of those late-bloomer types. You know, the kind of guy who takes his time finding a girl who will turn him on. But I think he's just about due to meet someone who's going to knock his socks off."

Well, it was an interesting theory all right, and if anyone could speak with authority about love and romance, it was Christabel Collins.

We drove back to the hostel in the Holmbergs' blue minivan, which they'd lent us for the evening.

As we came down the last half mile of road, we saw that a police roadblock had been erected: a wooden barricade flanked by a pair of police cars, their red lights flashing.

Ron rolled down the window on the driver's side of the van and stuck his head out.

"What's up, Officer?"

Two policemen came over to the van, one on each side, and played the beams of their flashlights over all of us.

Chip and Melanie straightened up hastily in the backseat. I saw Melanie try to pat her hair back in place.

"We're staying at the hostel down the road," James said. "Has there been any trouble?"

The policeman at the driver's window pushed his Smokey the Bear hat back on his head and replied, "No, not exactly. We're look-ing for someone, though. You kids didn't see an old guy in a red flannel shirt and khaki pants walking along the road, did you?"

"No," Ron said. "Has he committed some crime?"

"Not unless you consider being crazy as a bedbug a crime. His name's Amos Fletcher, and he used to live around here. He grew up on this river."

"Used to live?" I heard myself asking.

"Yeah, until his relatives had him certified as insane and committed to the state mental hospi-tal. That was a few years ago, and now Amos has gone and busted out of the hospital. We figure he's headed this way. This area is the only home he knows, and the doctors said he was always talking about coming back."

"Oh great," Christabel moaned. "That's all we need—a nutball roaming around. Is he dan-gerous?"

The policeman scratched his head. "He didn't used to be. But he did get kind of carried away there, just before he escaped."

"Carried away?" Christabel, the queen, had assumed control. "What do you mean, *carried away*?"

"Well, he took a knife to a guy who worked with him. Amos had been given a trustee job in the kitchen. Everyone thought he was better. I guess he'd fooled them."

"Did he kill the guy in the kitchen?" Ron asked.

"No, but the fella needed a few stitches afterward."

"Oh, God," Christabel said. "Jack the Ripper strikes again!"

"Now, now, miss," the policeman said soothingly. "It's not as bad as it sounds. That fella in the kitchen really provoked Amos. He asked for it, from what we hear. Amos isn't bad. Just a little excitable."

"Wonderful," Christabel said sarcastically. "That makes everything okay. I should have known. We're in the country, and this is what passes for local color."

I was hanging over the front seat. I saw Ron elbow Christabel in an effort to make her shut up. For once she took the hint.

James leaned forward. He was sitting beside me in the middle row of the van. "We'll keep a lookout for him, Officer," he said politely. I could tell he was trying to make up for Christabel's rudeness. "Is there anything special we should do if we find him?"

"Just don't try to be heroes or anything," the policeman replied. "Don't try to apprehend him. Humor him along if you meet him face-to-face. Then get to a phone and call us. We know how to handle old Amos."

The police removed the barricades and motioned us through.

"I can see," Melanie groaned as we resumed speed, "that I'm really going to earn these extra credits. What if this Amos creature is lurking around the hostel?"

"Don't worry, Melanie. I'll defend you," Chip said happily.

"He's probably miles from here," Tracy said. "After being cooped up in a hospital all those years, I'm sure being around a bunch of teenagers is the last thing he wants."

"Well I, for one, am not going to worry about it," I declared. "I'm sure we're perfectly safe, and besides, we're leaving tomorrow morning for Shadow Island. I'm going to get a good night's sleep."

But I didn't. I'd wake up every now and then and wonder about Amos Fletcher. What was it like to be locked up in an institution for years and years? James had been in a hospital when he'd been treated for depression. Did he have any idea how Amos felt? And how *did* Amos feel now? Was he simply happy to be free, or was he wandering the area, bent on some twisted revenge?

FOUR

I was already in the kitchen the next morning when Tracy entered.

"Where are the Holmbergs?" she asked, yawning. "You'd think they'd be down here taking charge."

"It *is* strange," I agreed. "I'll go look for them in a minute. Where's everyone else?"

"Christabel and Melanie are getting all put together for the trip. Honestly, Angie, you'd think they were primping for a screen test. I heard the guys making plans last night to carry all our gear down to the boat house before breakfast. They'll probably be finished soon."

The boat house was a few yards from the hostel, down on the riverbank. Mr. Holmberg had made arrangements for the rental of the four canoes we'd be needing for the trip.

I was laying out cereal bowls and plates on the long pine table when I heard the guys stomping up the steps of the back porch.

"Maybe we'd better not tell the girls," Ron was saying.

"Good idea," Chip agreed. "It would only scare them."

"Better not tell the girls what?" I asked as they shouldered their way through the door.

"Yeah, what?" Christabel had just come into the kitchen. She was wearing tight jeans and a lime-colored T-shirt. Her hair was pulled back from her face with a matching ribbon. "Come on, Ron. You know you can't keep a secret from me."

The three boys exchanged glances. Then James shrugged and said, "The man at the boat house told us someone broke in and stole a canoe last night."

"So what?" Christabel began. "Why all the hush-hush stuff?" she asked, pausing. "Oh! Oh, no! You mean you think that maybe it was—"

"Amos?" Tracy put in. "Do you think maybe Amos was around here last night?"

Melanie came into the kitchen with a little

shriek. She liked to make dramatic entrances. "Amos? That awful old man was here last night?"

Chip was at her side in two manly strides. "Don't worry, Mel. If he was, he's gone now."

"Why do you think he wanted a boat?" Tracy asked. "Where's he going in it?"

"That's a good question, Tracy," I said. "The police said he was from around here. Where would he be headed?"

"Not to Shadow Island, I hope," Christabel said with a shiver.

"Of course not." James sounded impatient. "Why should he? He's probably gone downriver and is holed up somewhere until the police stop looking for him."

"Well, I hope we don't meet up with him," I said.

"I'm sure we won't," James assured me. "The poor guy probably just wants to be alone out in the woods after being cooped up and treated like a sickie for years."

He said this with such fervor that, again, I wondered what he had experienced during those weeks when he'd been undergoing treatment for his depression. Was this why he acted like such a loner at times?

"James is right," I agreed. "I guess we should forget about Amos Fletcher and eat some breakfast."

"Good idea," Ron said. "I'm so hungry I could eat a"—he glanced down at the table—"cornflake."

We were sitting around the table, finishing breakfast, when Mrs. Holmberg tottered into the kitchen.

That was the only word for it. Tottered.

She looked terrible. Her face was ashen, and her eyes were sunken and black-ringed. Her hair was uncombed, and she wore a plaid flannel bathrobe, which she modestly clutched about her slender body.

This was a Mrs. Holmberg none of us had ever seen before.

"Oh dear," she moaned. "Philip and I are so terribly sick."

Ron jumped up and helped her into his seat. "What is it?"

Mrs. Holmberg took a crumpled handkerchief from her bathrobe pocket and wiped her brow with a trembling hand. She was perspiring profusely.

"I can only stay a moment. I . . . I must get back to bed. I feel so dizzy."

"What about Mr. Holmberg?" I asked. "Is he all right?"

"He's resting. For the moment. But we have been up all night." She was almost weeping. "All night. Oh, it was terrible! And it still afflicts us!"

I bit back a smile. It wasn't that I didn't feel sorry for Mrs. Holmberg. It was just that she was acting like a hammy Shakespearean actress about her mysterious problem.

"What afflicts you?" James asked, puzzled.

"I really can't explain in detail," Mrs. Holmberg replied, blushing. "I've called a local doctor, and he says we have an extremely distressing intestinal affliction that's going around."

"Oh, *that* kind of affliction!" Christabel said, with an arch glance at Melanie. They looked as if they were about to burst out laughing.

"And since we are unable at this point to go too far from . . . uh, to accompany you on an extended canoe trip"—she paused and shuddered—"we feel—Philip and I—that you should stay here until we fully recover."

"You mean not go to Shadow Island?" Chip asked.

39

"Not until you can be properly chaperoned," Mrs. Holmberg said primly.

"Mrs. Holmberg," Chip began, "that chaperon stuff's for little kids. We don't need chaperons. Why can't we go on ahead and wait for you and Mr. Holmberg on the island?"

"I'm sorry, my dear, but—"

"This isn't a pleasure trip, you know," Ron said, taking charge and slipping Chip an almost invisible wink. "It's a scientific expedition. We're getting extra credit for it, and we'd all be very disappointed if we weren't allowed to have our full week of studying the flora and fauna of Shadow Island."

"That's right," Chip put in eagerly. "I've really been looking forward to learning more about . . . biology!"

James looked over at me, raised his eyebrows, and shrugged expressively.

"But—but—the canoe trip," Mrs. Holmberg argued. "Philip said you couldn't manage without him!"

"I happen to be a certified Water Safety Instructor," Ron said. "And a qualified canoeist. I'd be happy to take full responsibility for the trip."

40

"And I've been a lifeguard for two summers," Chip said.

"We're all good swimmers, Mrs. Holmberg," Christabel added. "We'll be perfectly safe."

Mrs. Holmberg wrung her hands. "Oh dear, I don't know what to say. If only Philip were well enough to come down here and talk to you."

"Maybe we *should* talk this over more," I began timidly. "Maybe we should wait until—"

Christabel shot me a look of poisonous disbelief. "Shut up!" she mouthed silently.

Melanie scowled at me. If looks could kill, I'd have been struck dead on the spot.

Tracy put a hand over her mouth to smother a giggle.

"But then again, on the other hand," I amended hastily, "as Christabel says, we'll be perfectly safe. I mean, we're all swimmers and everything. . . . Tracy's even got a swimming scholarship to Stanford . . . she's awfully good, you know, and . . ."

"I agree with Angie," James interrupted. "There's no reason for us to postpone the trip, Mrs. Holmberg. We can get there ahead of you and Mr. Holmberg and set everything up in the cabin for you."

41

Mrs. Holmberg rose from her chair, a look of acute distress on her face.

"But . . . but . . . ," she protested.

"Don't worry about anything, Mrs. Holmberg," Ron said smoothly. "You and Mr. Holmberg just concentrate on getting better. Fluids. Bed rest. You know."

Mrs. Holmberg moaned softly and ran from the room.

"Does that mean yes or no?" I asked.

"I think it means yes," Chip said, "but let's get out of here before she changes her mind. Fantasy Island, here we come!"

Christabel wheeled on me, her face flushed and angry. "If you ever pull something like that again, Angie, you can forget about hanging out with me. Don't you ever, *ever* mess things up for us the way you almost did just now, okay?"

"Okay," I said, puzzled by her nastiness. "I . . . I didn't realize . . ."

"Well now you do, so watch your step!"

"The canoes are loaded," said James. "Are you girls ready?"

"I brought my backpack with me when I came downstairs for breakfast," Tracy said. "It's on the porch with Angie's."

"Melanie's and mine are there, too," Christabel said.

"What are we waiting for?" Chip said. "I give the Holmbergs forty-eight hours, max, to get over their illness. And then they'll be on us like fleas on a dog. So, as they say in all the old cowboy movies, let's vamoose, muchachos!"

We vamoosed.

FIVE

It was cold on the river.

It was the end of April, but spring comes late to that part of Vermont. I was glad I was wearing a heavy sweater.

The sun, which had been shining in full force the day before, was now hiding behind thick, dark clouds.

"It looks like rain," Ron called to us.

The three canoes were traveling pretty much abreast, and we could talk back and forth between them.

"Maybe even a storm, the way the clouds look over in that direction," James said, pointing.

"That's what they predicted on TV," I said.

"Well, thanks a lot for sharing that fact with

us," Christabel snapped. She was still angry with me. "I wouldn't have come if I'd known a storm was on the way."

"You know that weathermen are wrong more times than they're right, Christabel," I soothed. "Besides, Mr. Holmberg never cancels a trip because of weather. And you said you needed this trip desperately."

That seemed to settle her down a bit.

What I would have liked to tell her—but didn't have the nerve—was that she could have easily checked on the weather herself. I knew she had her own color TV in her bedroom.

I'm glad she didn't check, though. This trip was important to me. I'd worked hard to be included in an outing like this with Christabel's crowd. I'd have hated to see the weekend canceled just because of a little rain.

It was one thing to sit with them in the cafeteria and at assemblies, and to be greeted in the halls as one of the clique. But to spend the weekend with them was something else, especially since I hadn't been friends with Christabel for very long. Being included on this trip was a major step up socially for me.

Some of the other kids from the gang at school had wanted to come on the trip to

Shadow Lake. It would have been all right with Mr. Holmberg. What did he know about the pecking order of Oakbridge High society?

But, unknown to him, Christabel was calling the shots on who would be going and who wouldn't. And she had particularly wanted me. True, it was mainly because I was a whiz in science. But nevertheless, here I was.

"Hey, wake up, Angie," James chided from behind me. "You're dragging your paddle."

"Sorry," I said, and paddled vigorously, splashing water back in his face. "There. Is that better?"

"I think I liked it better the other way," James said with a laugh.

"Hey, cut the clowning around back there," Tracy called lightly back over her shoulder. "Am I supposed to do all the work myself while the two of you perfect a comedy routine?"

"Sorry, Tracy!" James said, smiling and splashing her with water as well.

When we first set out down the Doone River, we'd paddled past small, isolated towns that bordered the water. Then, after we'd gone a few miles, civilization began to thin out, and we saw only the occasional farm.

But now that we'd been on the river for a

47

couple of hours, we were hitting long stretches of semiwilderness. Every once in a while we'd see an abandoned camp or a few dirt roads that paralleled the river, but the roads were narrow and ran for only short distances.

The sun came out, briefly, at one point, and since the water was running briskly, we drifted with the current.

I put my arms on my knees and watched lazily as we passed trees that seemed to bend out over the water. It was so lovely and peaceful. I wished the trip could go on forever.

"I didn't know you knew Michael Giddings," James said suddenly. His remark was abrupt and unexpected, and his voice sounded gruff and a little harsh.

I could feel my spine stiffen, but I managed to say, "Why should you? You and I didn't know each other very well until the beginning of this semester."

"I guess it really hurt when he . . . when he died." I don't know why James wanted to talk about Michael, but it made me uncomfortable.

"Yes," I answered. "We were pretty close."

We were so close, and so much alike, that I

knew what he was thinking even before he said it aloud.

"Yeah, come to think of it, I guess I *did* see the two of you together a lot in the halls."

"We had some classes together," I said. "Science classes."

Michael was a science nerd, like me, and as much a social outsider as I was. His was the loneliness of genius. And aren't all geniuses lonely because they are so much above everyone else? I felt privileged to be allowed to share his life and his loneliness.

The two of us moved quietly among the invisible untouchables of Oakbridge High. But I know this for certain—that, if he had lived, someday Michael would have done something important. For the world. Maybe he and I would have done it together.

But he was gone, so I did the next-best thing. For all his absentminded genius, Michael admired beauty. So I made myself beautiful for Michael. And I determined to make it for Michael in the most exclusive clique in school.

I was roused from my daydreaming by the loud, clear sound of birds singing.

It seemed as if it were coming from directly

behind me. I turned on my bench and looked over my shoulder.

James was holding something in his hand. A mini tape recorder.

"James?" I asked incredulously. "Where'd you get that crazy tape?"

"You mean you don't know I'm an audio freak, Angie? That disappoints me. I thought I was famous for it at Oakbridge High. These are some bird calls I recorded one afternoon when I was out with Mr. Holmberg."

"James really *is* an audio freak, you know," Tracy said. "He's always hovering around, picking up sounds with his trusty little tape recorder. I bet he's going to be a CIA agent someday."

"How interesting," I said, not really meaning it.

"Well," James said cheerfully. "We all have to have hobbies, don't we?"

"But why is yours so *boring*, James?" Tracy asked. "Why didn't you tape something we could really enjoy, like rap or something?"

"Because I'm a real intellectual-type guy, Tracy, in case you haven't noticed," James joked.

"Oh, give me a break," Tracy moaned.

"Look," I said, pointing. "The riverbank is getting higher and rockier."

Ahead, the banks were becoming bluffs, and the river appeared to be getting progressively deeper.

"What's happening?" I asked.

"The river's starting to move faster," Tracy answered. "That's because it's being channelized between the bluffs."

"Ooh, it's getting choppy," I said nervously. "I think this is where we separate the brave from the wimpy."

"You, wimpy, Angie?" James said in mock amazement. "I would have thought you were a real Valkyrie."

"A *what*?" asked Tracy.

"A female Viking," I said, clenching my teeth to keep them from chattering. We'd really picked up speed. "This is really scary."

"It's even scarier up here in the front seat," Tracy replied. She didn't sound a bit frightened, though. "And what's this female Viking stuff? I didn't know there were such things. I thought they were all male chauvinist pigs."

"If it's all the same to you, Tracy," I said, "I'd like to continue this discussion another time when I don't feel like screaming in terror!"

"Picky, picky," Tracy said.

Ron and Christabel's canoe was in the lead, with Melanie and Chip well behind us. I think Chip had lagged on purpose so he and Melanie could be alone, but now I saw them trying to close the gap.

"See that small river up there on the left?" Ron called out. "That's the Blye. We're going to turn onto it."

"Are you sure that's the right one?" James called back.

"Yeah. Mr. Holmberg and I went over the water route. That's the Blye all right. See that big cliff that looks like a man's head right above it? That's what we were supposed to look for."

I sat back on my bench and let out my breath. The Blye River. Finally. It looked narrow and comforting after the last rapidly moving section of the Doone.

The water didn't seem to be rushing and tumbling as hard here. There were bits of floating wood, but they were small and broken, old fallen pieces of trees, probably washed into the river by a rainstorm, and they didn't slow us down or hurt the canoes.

I saw why Mr. Holmberg hadn't wanted us to

go on without him. This trip—the part on the Doone, anyway—wasn't for beginners.

I was glad the guys and Tracy knew what they were doing. Although I'd been taught basic canoeing when I was young and learning water sports, I certainly wasn't an expert.

I hoped Mr. Holmberg wouldn't be too upset and unhappy with Mrs. Holmberg for not stopping us. We'd really taken advantage of her. Poor little thing. She was so sweet.

She couldn't have stopped us anyway, as determined as everyone was to have a couple of days on the island without adult supervision.

I wasn't surprised, though. I'd figured that Ron and Christabel, Chip and Melanie, would want to go on alone, and that they'd get their way. They always seemed to get their way.

Canoeing on the Blye wasn't as easy as I'd thought it would be. The little river wound tortuously around and about the bleak cliffs. The bits of floating debris had increased in number. We had to watch out for them and dodge the bigger ones.

"It looks like they've had some rain in this neck of the woods," Ron called out.

"And more on the way," James answered.

He was right. The skies were darkening ominously. To the north of us, a large black cloud had appeared and seemed to be moving slowly in our direction. I hoped we could make it to the cabin on Storm Lake before it began to pour.

It was early afternoon when we arrived at Shadow Island, but because of the darkness it seemed much later.

We'd just come around a bend that was flanked by two towering bluffs when the river dead-ended in Storm Lake.

The lake was large, several miles wide in all directions. Shadow Island sat directly in the middle, like a stone set in a ring. A black, opaque stone in a funereal ring.

"They really knew what they were doing when they named this place," Ron said as we approached the eastern side of the island, where there was a narrow wedge of sandy beach. "This will definitely *not* be a sun-filled holiday."

The sun, what little there was of it, was hidden behind the bluffs that loomed like grim guardians over the lake.

"If this is what it's going to be like all week," Christabel said, "I brought my new bikini for nothing."

"Don't worry, Christabel," Ron assured her. "A bikini is never wasted on you."

"Is it the sexy blue one with the brass rings, Chris?" Melanie asked.

"Yeah. I haven't worn it yet. I was saving it for the trip, but I didn't know it would be this cold up here."

Tracy looked over her shoulder at the approaching storm.

"If that bikini has brass rings on it, Chris, you'd better save it for a sunny day," she said. "In a thunderstorm, you'd be a walking lightning rod."

I choked back a giggle, but Christabel didn't seem to find the remark particularly funny. I really liked Tracy. Only she could get away with a crack like that.

The sight of the island seemed to act as a spur on the guys.

"Race you to the beach!" Chip called when we were about fifty yards from shore.

"You're on!" Ron shouted. "Paddle, Christabel!"

"Come on!" James urged. "Let's show them some muscle."

There was a flurry of hard paddling, with canoes colliding and water splashing.

"We win!" James yelled when we were only a couple of yards from shore. He leapt from the canoe and dragged it up on the rough, rocky sand.

"No fair!" Christabel squealed. "There were three of you and only two of us!"

"Might makes right," Tracy told her.

We all hopped out of the canoes and pushed them up on the beach.

When we'd caught our breath, we took a good look around.

Shadow Island looked even gloomier, once we were standing on the beach. The thick woods that began at the edge of the beach reminded me of something out of an old movie I'd seen once where a crazed scientist on a haunted island used shipwrecked sailors for ghastly experiments.

"If I were Tarzan," Tracy said, "I could swing from tree to tree across this entire island without my feet ever touching the ground."

"Forget Tarzan," Melanie said. "All we need is Jason coming out of the woods. I mean, I'm all for nature, but this is like *Friday the Thirteenth* come to life."

"We're seeing it on a bad day, Melanie," I said. "That's what makes it look so . . . bleak."

"I wonder if it ever *has* a good day," she replied. "All those trees, and it's so *dark*!"

"That's because it's going to rain soon," James said. "I think we ought to get our gear up to the cabin right away."

We pulled our canoes up as far as possible on the beach. Ron said we didn't want to chance them being blown out to the middle of the lake if high winds and rain made the lake water rise. We turned the canoes over, so they wouldn't accumulate rainwater, and stowed our life jackets beneath them. Then we gathered up our backpacks and other gear and started up the narrow pebble-strewn path that led to the cabin.

We couldn't see the cabin from the beach, although it was set on a rise that at one time must have looked out over the lake. Now it was heavily hemmed around with pine trees, growing crookedly and too close together.

We came up over the rise, and there sat the cabin.

We all stopped dead and looked at it. Silently. Dismally.

The cabin was old and seemed to list slightly in a westerly direction. Several floorboards were missing from the front steps, and the railing that enclosed the porch was broken off in sections. Several windowpanes gaped jaggedly.

"I think I'm going to scream," Christabel said in a high, tight voice. "Yes, I'm definitely going to scream."

"It might not be all that bad inside," Ron said, trying to calm her.

"But why didn't someone warn us about this . . . this . . . hellhole?"

"I think Cindy Morris tried," I said. "She said we'd be roughing it."

"Roughing it?" Christabel's eyes were blue ice. Her voice rose a decibel higher. "This is what she calls *roughing it*? To me, roughing it means living in a cute, clean little log cabin with early-American furniture. I thought that was what she meant by *roughing it*!"

The black clouds that we had seen all day seemed to grow even darker. I shivered. The temperature was dropping, and the wind was beginning to howl. I could see the branches of the trees moving back and forth. I shivered again. My mother has this old saying, that when you shiver, it means a goose has just walked across your grave. Standing there on that terrible island, I knew what she meant.

"Let's go inside," I said. "We're going to have to spend the night here whether we like it or not."

"What a little optimist," murmured Melanie. "And aren't we lucky to have her with us on this trip?"

"Back off, Melanie," Ron commanded. "How about getting off Angie's case for a change? You can be a real pain in the neck sometimes."

I flashed Ron a grateful smile. I was surprised to have him defending me, although I'd often suspected he didn't like Melanie. I wondered if he put up with her only because she was Christabel's best friend.

We walked up the steps, taking care not to put our feet down too hard, in case the boards were rotten.

Tracy entered the cabin first. The rest of us trailed her in various stages of reluctance and dread.

"This is unbelievable!" she said. "I bet this place is haunted!"

Six

Something rustled in a far corner. Something small and furtive. I told myself it was just a leaf, fluttering in the draft of the open door, but knew I was only kidding myself.

"I'll bet it has mice, though," I said, shuddering. "I'd rather face a ghost than a mouse."

"Don't worry, Angie," James said. "If there are any mice in here, they'll clear out right away. They're more scared of us than we are of them."

"I sure hope *they* know that," I said.

"Eeugh!" Christabel made a sour face. "Look at all the spiderwebs! And they've all got dead flies and bugs caught in them!"

"The mark of the vampire spider," Tracy said, speaking in a Count Dracula voice. She spread her arms out wide as if she were wearing a cape. "They trap their victims and then they drink their blooood!"

"Stop it, Tracy," Christabel snapped. "I don't think that's funny. This place is bad enough without you trying to spook us."

"Sorry," Tracy said with a grin. "I'll knock all those spiderwebs down for you, Chris, just as soon as I find a broom, some garlic, and a silver cross."

I bounced cautiously up and down on one foot, testing the floor. It squeaked and dipped. "Don't anybody tap-dance on this floor. It's pretty creaky and rotten. You might fall through."

"Great," Christabel said. "This is really great."

She turned to Ron and said, "And you told me this was going to be a real romantic weekend. The lake, the moon through the trees, and all that. I must have been crazy to listen to you."

"But . . . but, Chris," Ron protested. "It wasn't my fault. You said you *had* to come, because of your grades. How was I supposed to know it would be like this?"

Christabel didn't answer. She turned her back on him and stared sulkily around her.

The cabin had only three rooms. We were standing in a large *L*-shaped room, which was evidently the living and dining area.

A huge stone fireplace dominated the long end of the room. From the looks of things, it was used for cooking. It had a swing-out arm that held a teakettle. A three-legged iron "spider," upon which a cast-iron frying pan had been placed, straddled the fire. Both the pan and the kettle looked ancient. I was glad we'd brought our own cooking utensils, as well as canned goods and packets of dehydrated foods.

A couple of armchairs and a rocker faced the fireplace. On the opposite wall, a sagging sofa and two wicker chairs were clumped around an old coffee table.

Along the short end of the *L* was a rough wooden trestle table and chairs. A worktable, some overhead shelves, and a rather primitive-looking sink with a small, old-fashioned pump were the only other items in the dining area. "Dining" seemed far too elegant a word for it. A kerosene lamp stood on the table; the cabin didn't have electricity.

Christabel wandered over to the kitchen area

and stared at it in disbelief. "If this is the kitchen, I'm going to hate the bathroom!"

"I've got some bad news for you, Chris," Tracy said, returning from a short exploration of the cabin. "There *is* no bathroom."

"What do you mean, no bathroom?"

"I think I saw a little outhouse at the edge of the woods," I ventured helpfully.

"Then where am I expected to shower and wash my hair?" Christabel demanded.

"The lake, I guess," I said, "even though it's pretty cold right now. Or we can heat a bucket of water, maybe."

"Bathe in a bucket? If Mr. Holmberg doesn't die of his 'affliction,' I'm going to kill him myself," Christabel said.

"I have a feeling this is going to be a week to remember," Tracy said.

"I think I saw a place like this once in a horror movie," Melanie said. She glanced over at the fireplace and uttered a shrill scream. "Look! There's an animal on the mantel!"

We looked. Something dusty and horribly ugly crouched on the mantelpiece. It wasn't moving, but it was definitely a creature from the wild woodland.

Ron went over to it and examined it. He picked it up. It still didn't move.

"It's a stuffed owl," he said.

"A stuffed owl?" Christabel sounded as if she'd just reached her breaking point. "Oh, that's great. Maybe there's a crazy taxidermist running around the island."

"Just like Norman Bates in *Psycho*," Tracy added. "I wonder if we'll get to meet his dear old mother."

"Cut it out, Tracy," Melanie snapped. "This isn't the least bit funny."

"I wonder who brought a stuffed owl into this place," Ron said.

"The interior decorator, of course," Christabel snarled. "It completes the ambience of the room. Perfectly."

The remaining two rooms were placed one on each end of the *L*.

"Girls in one, boys in the other," Tracy pointed out. "With a big no-man's-land in the middle."

"Does this mean no hanky-panky after lights out?" Chip asked.

"Forget it, Romeo," Melanie said. "I've got a headache."

The bedrooms were rather small, with metal bunk beds along three walls.

"Three lowers and three uppers," I said. "Do we flip a coin to see which of us has to sleep in the upper?"

"Well, count me out," Christabel said. "This one down here's mine."

She had picked the only one with decent springs. No one said a word. Naturally.

"I'll take the upper," Tracy volunteered. "Maybe the dust won't be as bad up here. You know how my allergies kick up when there's a lot of dust."

"Well, I hope you brought pills or something with you," Christabel said crossly. "If you're going to sneeze and honk all night, we'll never get any sleep."

"I sure did," Tracy replied cheerfully. "I brought my nasal spray. It's right here in my little blue bag. I'll even hang it on the bedstead so I can get to it at night without climbing down over you."

"You are *too* kind," Christabel said.

"Break it up, girls," James called to us. "It's starting to drizzle out there. We've got a lot to do before the rain starts coming down hard."

"Our fearless leader calls," Tracy said. I had a

feeling she was enjoying Christabel's and Melanie's discomfort.

I wondered, not for the first time, why Tracy even bothered with the other girls. She always seemed to be secretly laughing at them. Was it because of James, or did she have some other reason?

Tracy and I usually sat by each other in the cafeteria, and I think she liked me as much as I liked her, but she was a private person. Maybe "independent" is more the right word. She didn't seem to care what people thought about her and tended to keep her thoughts to herself. So even though I'd tried to get close to her, it was impossible. She was always warm and friendly—and funny—but she never let you know how she really felt about things.

"So what do you want us to do, James?" Tracy asked. "I want an easy job."

It was strange to see James stepping in and taking charge. Ron was usually the one who took charge, in his unquestioned role as captain of the football team and class president who ran the show. But Ron was a little out of it right now, what with Christabel sulking and acting as if the awful cabin and terrible weather were his fault.

Didn't he know how spoiled Christabel was? That she was like a child, and if she wasn't having a good time she'd find someone to blame for it? I had a feeling Ron would get to know a lot about Christabel on this trip.

"We're going to need plenty of firewood," James was saying. "It'll get cold in here tonight. We'll need logs and smaller bits of wood for kindling. We'd better get it right now while it's still relatively dry."

"How much do we need?" Christabel demanded. "How many of us have to go? I don't want to go out there and get wet."

"Me neither," chimed in Melanie.

"Good," James said. "Then you've just volunteered for cabin-cleaning duty. I wondered who I could get. There are brooms out in the shed. This place needs a good sweeping down. Oh, and while you're at it, one of you will have to go down the little path there and check out the outhouse."

"*Outhouse?*" Christabel gasped. "You're asking us to actually *clean* that thing?"

"Not for a white-glove inspection or anything, Chris," James said. "But you'll have to take a broom and knock down spiderwebs and sweep out old leaves and stuff."

"I will not!" Christabel said. "I'll go gather firewood. Tracy, you can have cabin duty. You're not afraid of spiders and creepy crawlers."

"My allergies, remember?" Tracy said. "You don't want me sneezing and honking all night, do you?"

"Here, Chris, I'll leave something to cheer you and Melanie up," James said.

He laid his tape recorder on the mantel and pressed the "on" button.

The theme from *Rocky* immediately started up, played with lots of tootling and squeaking and sour notes.

"Don't tell me you actually recorded the Oakbridge High orchestra?" I asked.

"Right. Wherever musical history is being made, there I am with my tape recorder."

"No wonder they put him away," Christabel said when James was out of earshot. "They shouldn't have let him out. Personally, I think he's still crazy."

Tracy, Ron, Chip, and I set out to bring in the firewood. James said he'd fix the kitchen pump and straighten up the shed. There were lots of things out there, he said, that we could use in the cabin.

The four of us wood-gatherers split up. Ron and Chip were to get the larger logs. Tracy and I carried plastic garbage bags for the small sticks and bits of fallen branches we'd need for kindling.

It had begun to rain when we started, not hard, but enough to indicate more was on the way.

The woods had turned dark. Threateningly dark. I was reminded of all the awful, bloody fairy tales I'd read as a child—stories about children dying in the forest and wicked stepmothers trying to poison beautiful stepdaughters.

I was the last to return from the woods.

Well, next to last.

Chip was still out there.

By now it had begun to rain harder, pounding down on the tin roof of the cabin. The wind had started up, too, and was moaning around the chimney like an unhappy ghost. The cabin was growing dim. We would soon have to light an oil lamp to hold back the darkness.

"Where's Chip?" James asked. "Has anyone seen him?"

"He was in the wooded area down by the

70

beach when I last saw him," Ron said. "I can't imagine why he's still out there."

"Maybe he's trying to cool off out there in the rain," Tracy said. "Melanie *did* tell him she had a headache."

"I hate it when you act smart, Tracy," Melanie said. "And where *is* Chip? He should be here by now."

"Maybe I should go out and look for him," Ron suggested.

"Well, someone should do *something*," Christabel snapped. "Maybe Chip needs help carrying wood."

"Yeah," Ron said. "Maybe."

Ron was acting like an entirely different person from the one I was used to seeing at school. Christabel's put-downs were getting to him, cutting him off at the knees and leaving him off balance and uncertain. She was pretty good at doing that.

"I'll go with you, Ron," James offered.

"Me too," I said. "The more the merrier. And besides, I've got naturally curly hair. I scoff at rain."

"Wait for me," Tracy said. "Maybe this will count as a bath."

As it turned out, we all went to look for Chip.

Nobody wanted to stay in the cabin alone. There was something oppressive and sinister about the surrounding woods, and everyone seemed to sense it. Maybe we'd all seen too many creepy movies on TV—you know, where you hear heavy breathing and footsteps crunching on fallen leaves and then somebody gets knifed. Anyway, we all went as a group, to look for Chip.

We headed in the direction Ron had indicated—the wooded area down by the beach.

"Chip!" we called as we crashed through the woods. "Chip!"

No one answered. There was only the sound of the wind whipping the branches of the trees.

"Chip!"

We finally found him.

Chip was lying on his face.

He was still. Too still.

"Is he passed out or what?" Ron asked.

It wasn't until we gathered around him that we noticed the large clot of blood that darkened the blond hair on the back of his skull.

"He's hurt!" Melanie sobbed. "Oh, Chip!"

Ron and James gently rolled Chip on his back. His eyes were open, but there was no flicker of movement in them.

"Why isn't he moving?" Melanie whispered. "What are you doing, James?"

James didn't answer. He bent over Chip and tried to give him mouth-to-mouth resuscitation.

We watched in horrid fascination.

Finally James leaned back and rubbed his eyes.

"It's no use," he said. "He's dead."

Melanie took a step backward. She was so pale, I was afraid she was going to faint.

"No. No, not Chip! He can't be!" She appealed to Ron. "He's not dead, is he, Ron?"

Ron seemed unable to answer.

It was Christabel who said, "Yes, Melanie. Chip's dead."

"But . . . but how?" Melanie was sobbing now.

James and Chip were still kneeling over the body.

"How?" Melanie repeated.

James looked up. "He must have slipped and fallen."

"But his head . . . the blood on his head! All that blood!" Melanie moaned.

"I guess he hit his head on a rock when he fell." James's voice wavered a little. He sounded uncertain.

Ron was as quiet and unmoving as Chip's body. He seemed to be in a state of shock. Tears were running down his cheeks, but he made no effort to wipe them away.

"He fell and hit his head hard enough to kill himself?" I asked.

"What else could it be?" James replied.

"What rock? Where's the rock?" I asked. "I don't see any rock."

"Oh for God's sake, Angie!" Christabel said. "What difference does that make now?" She had her arm around Melanie, who was weeping uncontrollably.

I ignored her. "But it's important, James. If he accidentally killed himself, it ought to be obvious how he did it. Where's the rock?"

James looked around. Then he pointed. "There. The one with the blood on it. It has to be the one."

The rock was a few feet away from Chip's body.

I shuddered. "Yes, I see. But how could he hit his head on it and land over here?"

"I don't know. It must have happened that way, though."

"But, James . . ."

Tracy put her hand on my shoulder. She gave

74

me a warning pinch and signaled me to be quiet with an almost imperceptible jerk of her head toward Melanie and Christabel.

"Give it a rest," she said in a low, almost inaudible tone. "Those two are going to lose it completely."

Then, aloud, she said firmly, "Chip slipped and hit his head, Angie. There's no other possible explanation."

But Christabel had heard enough to make her forget, for a moment, the sobbing Melanie.

"What do you mean?" she demanded. "What's all this crap about Chip being too far away from the rock to hit his head on it?"

"Nothing," James said. "It's nothing."

I looked down at my feet.

"You're hiding something," Christabel accused. "I can tell."

Neither James nor I replied.

"Are you trying to say it wasn't an accident?"

"We're not trying to say anything, Christabel," James assured her.

Melanie stopped sobbing and rounded on James and me. Her mascara had begun to run. Long black lines were zigzagging down her cheeks, making trails in her blusher.

"What the hell's the matter with you people?

Chip's dead! Why are you making a big mystery of it? Are you crazy or something? If Chip didn't hit his head when he fell, then someone had to do it to him, is that what you're saying?"

"No, Melanie, of course not," James said hastily.

"Oh yes you are!"

Her eyes were red and glaring.

"You're saying Chip didn't die accidentally. That someone *murdered* him!"

SEVEN

We had to do something with Chip's body.

We carried it home through the rain and placed it in the shed, covering it with a poncho.

It was hard to believe that, just a few hours before, the still, icy form on the floor of the shed had been a real person, full of life and laughter.

We were all silent with horror and shock as we closed the door on the shrouded body.

James and I had managed to convince Melanie that no one was saying Chip had been murdered.

"Forget what we said when we found Chip's body, Melanie," James said. "We were all a little out of it and talking crazy."

Melanie couldn't stop trembling and crying

uncontrollably when we reached the cabin. Christabel took her into the bedroom, helped her change into a warm, dry sweatshirt and sweatpants, and tucked her into her sleeping bag. This seemed to settle Melanie a little, and she was soon asleep.

It was a good thing we'd returned to the cabin when we did. As soon as we were inside, the rain began to bucket down, and the wind increased in velocity, whipping the rain against the walls of the cabin.

Ron and James ran out on the porch and closed the shutters, while Tracy and I got a fire going in the fireplace. There were a few old dry logs in the basket by the hearth, and we had fire starters in addition to the kindling.

Then we made a pot of strong coffee. We figured everyone would need it. We made it pioneer style, setting the pot on the three-legged iron "spider" and shoving it up against the flames.

Christabel even helped, fumbling around with a can opener and scraping a few cans of chili into a large kettle, which we hung from the swing-out arm over the fire.

Under normal circumstances it would have been a cheerful scene—a crackling fire, with the delicious smells of coffee perking and chili simmering. It was ironic that what was supposed to have been a romantic evening had turned into a tragedy for Chip, the one who'd had his heart set on a romantic getaway.

There was no chance of leaving the island tonight. With the storm and the darkness, we'd never make it back upriver to the hostel.

No one had much to say as we sat before the fire, drinking our coffee. Ron, in particular, had seemed silent and distant since we'd returned to the cabin. He and Chip had been close friends since they were little kids, and now he seemed to be in a terrible state of shock.

"I wonder how long this rain's going to keep up," Tracy said. "It's giving me the willies."

"Me too," I said. "I keep thinking of Chip out there in that cold shed, all alone."

"Didn't anyone bring a radio, so we can listen to the weather report?" Christabel asked. "What about you, James? You're usually the one with all the audio equipment."

"I only brought my tape recorder," he told her. "I figured Mr. Holmberg would bring a radio. He always thinks of everything. He even packed a CB radio in case of an emergency."

"Then why didn't somebody think to bring it

with us?" Christabel demanded. "If this isn't an emergency, I don't know what is."

"We left in a hurry, remember?" Tracy said. "We wanted a couple of days on this island without chaperons."

"Chip was the one who wanted us to be alone out here," Ron said, rousing himself from his silence. "And look where it got him. Dead."

His eyes filled with tears, and he knuckled them away with trembling hands. "Chip was my best friend, and now he's dead."

"Get a grip, Ron." Christabel's tone was severe. "What happened to Chip was an accident. It could have happened anywhere."

"Accident? He slipped and hit his head, is that what you're all thinking?"

Ron paused and looked searchingly at each of our faces.

"Well, if that's so, then explain this to me. How come he landed facedown?"

"What?" Christabel asked. "What are you talking about?"

"We found Chip facedown. But it was the back of his head that was all busted up. How'd he do that? If he slipped and hit the back of his head, wouldn't he be lying on his *back*?"

"Oh no!" Christabel said. "Don't tell me that

now *you're* trying to say Chip's death wasn't an accident! So what was it? Murder? Are you trying to tell us that somebody on this island murdered Chip? That's the stupidest thing you've ever said, Ron."

James rose and stood by the mantel. "I think we'd all better chill out. Melanie can hear us in there"—he indicated the bedroom with a jerk of his head—"and she's in pretty bad shape. If she hears what you're saying, Ron, she's going to come unglued."

"So what are we supposed to do?" Ron asked contemptuously. "Just pass it off as if nothing's happened?"

"No. What I'm saying is, let's make it through the night somehow and then tomorrow, at first light, get in our canoes and beat it out of here."

"But what about the . . . the . . . body?" I asked.

"We'll have to leave it here. When we get to the hostel, we'll call the police. They'll send a team out for it. And in the meantime we'll tell them everything we can about Chip's death. They'll have to figure out what happened, not us."

We all agreed that was the only thing we

could do, and settled back and ate our chili. I was surprised anyone could eat anything, but we managed to empty the entire pot.

Melanie got up and joined us for a little while. She looked awful, but must have been feeling better, because she was her old bitchy self again, criticizing and demanding.

"I've got to go to the john, but I'm scared to go alone," she whined.

Christabel and Tracy said they'd take her, and they headed off through the wind and rain, to the little house at the edge of the woods.

They came back sopping wet and complaining, of course, about how primitive life was on the island.

We all went to bed early. We were more tired than we'd realized. It had been a day no one wished to prolong, and we'd have to get up early the next morning.

I'd put off my trip to the outhouse until the last possible moment. Now that I was ready to go, everyone was asleep, and I'd have to go out by myself.

I pulled my poncho on, jammed a rain hat down over my ears, and picked up a flashlight.

The trees that lined the path hid the moonlight, and I had to keep playing the beam of the flashlight on the ground ahead of me for fear of twisting my ankle on a rock or tree root. I couldn't hear anything—only the wind—and I thought, with a quick look behind me, that someone could easily creep up on me.

The force of the wind took my breath away. I was facing into it and had to lean forward, clutching my poncho around me, to keep it from fluttering backward.

Returning to the cabin, I had to endure the wind at my back, pushing me along.

I could hear the high winds kicking up the lake below, and the waves it caused were splashing up against the beachline. They almost sounded like incoming waves at a seashore.

The night air was cold. I shivered. I thought of Chip's body out there in that dirty shed and wondered if it was true that people's spirits hang around the place they'd died before moving on to wherever it is they finally go. Was Chip here, in the woods? No, I decided. If he was anywhere, he was hanging around the football field at Oakbridge High. That was more his style.

The wind was blowing from a northwest direction, across the island and out over the water. There was a gap in the trees. I clung to a small pine tree to keep my balance and looked down at the lake.

The moon was full, but little rags of driven clouds kept fluttering past it, making its light wink on and off like a signal lantern.

I wondered about the canoes. If they weren't secured properly, they could be washed off the beach and out across the lake. And then we'd be stuck on this miserable island until the Holmbergs came paddling to the rescue. Considering the shape they were in, they wouldn't be doing any paddling for at least another twenty-four hours, if that soon.

But Ron had known what he was doing, hadn't he? He'd pulled the canoes way up on the beach, where neither the wind nor the rain could possibly get at them.

I slept soundly that night.

We all awoke at first light the next morning.

It was still raining, but it was only a mild, steady patter, not the hard, driving sheets we'd had the night before.

The wind hadn't blown itself out yet, either, but was nearly spent, gusting only occasionally, just often enough to let us know it was still around.

I was dressed and ready ahead of the other girls. Tracy was having a hard time getting out of bed, and Christabel and Melanie were making a pitiful stab at putting on their faces and fixing their hair. Without electricity and modern plumbing, it was pretty difficult.

I wondered for whom Melanie was putting on makeup now, with Chip gone. And Christabel—did she still want to charm Ron? I doubted it. The way she was treating him, their romance definitely looked on the rocks to me. I guessed this grooming thing was a compulsion with them, like salmon that simply *must* swim upstream to their breeding grounds, even if they don't have any special Significant Other in mind.

I had the fire going again and was brewing a pot of coffee when Tracy appeared. She was sleepy-eyed but cheerful and began laying out fruit and boxes of breakfast cereal on the long trestle table.

I saw her absentmindedly set a seventh cereal bowl and spoon on the table and then hastily snatch them back up, a look of horror on her face, as she realized the seventh member of our party would not be coming in to breakfast.

James and Ron appeared and ate quickly.

"I'll get all the gear together and carry it down to the beach," James said. "I'll need some help from you all, though."

"Fine," I replied. "My stuff's ready to go right now."

Ron stood up and wiped his mouth with a paper napkin. "And I'll go check out the canoes. I don't think the storm could have damaged them, but I'll get them turned right side up and ready for loading."

"We'll only need two this time," James reminded him. "We'll worry about bringing the third one back later."

"Yeah," said Ron. "Melanie will have to go with Christabel and me. But all our gear won't fit in just two canoes."

"Then we'd better load the essentials first. The police can bring the rest back later," James said.

Melanie and Christabel wandered in after Ron had left. Melanie looked pretty terrible. Her eyes were swollen and puffy from all the crying she'd done the night before.

Christabel had cast herself in the role of Florence Nightingale and was doing her sympathetic nurse routine on Melanie.

"We'll be on our way home soon," she was

telling Melanie. "And then we'll put this terrible thing behind us."

Heavy footsteps were heard on the porch, and Ron flung the door open.

His face was ashen.

"The canoes!" he gasped. "They're gone!"

EIGHT

Christabel was the first to find her voice.

"What do you mean, *gone*?"

"The canoes!" Ron repeated breathlessly. "They're not on the beach!"

"Oh, God!" Melanie moaned.

"So where are they? Have they been stolen?" Christabel's voice was shrill.

"No," Ron said, "not stolen. The waves must have come up on the beach and swept them out into the water."

"Can you see them?" James asked.

"Yeah, on the far side of the lake," Ron answered grimly. "The wind's blown them clear across."

"I thought you'd beached them where they'd

be secure," Christabel snapped. "You're supposed to be our big boating expert!"

Ron looked puzzled. "But I did. I knew a storm was coming, so I pulled them far enough up on the beach that they couldn't be washed out."

"Well, obviously that wasn't far enough, was it?"

Christabel looked at Ron with open hostility. Gone was the teasing love-goddess personality she used to assume with him. I noticed with some satisfaction that she didn't look so pretty in the early-morning light. She looked hard.

"I think we ought to go down to the beach and have a look," James said. "Maybe there's something we can do."

We grabbed our ponchos and headed for the lake.

The pebbles on the path were slick from the rain, and little potholes along the way were filled, ankle deep, with water. I wondered if, when this was over, I'd ever feel dry again. My jeans were moldy and damp, and my turtleneck pullover clung to my body like a dishrag.

The beach was bare, just as Ron had said.

"Nothing, not even a life jacket," I said. "How could that be?"

James gave me a sharp look. "That's right. There were life jackets, seven of them, under the canoes. Surely at least one of them would be floating close to shore."

"I overturned the canoes when I left them on the beach," Ron said. "I'd say it was almost impossible for either them or the life jackets to have been swept away like that."

"Impossible or not, it happened," Christabel said. "So what are we supposed to do now, Mr. Expert?"

"Oh, give it a rest, Chris," Ron pleaded. "Enough's enough. And I'm tired of hearing your voice!"

Christabel gaped at Ron, openmouthed. No one ever spoke to Her Highness in those tones.

"Where are the canoes, Ron? I can't see them," I said, squinting.

Ron pointed to the opposite side of the lake. "Over there."

I looked again. Yes, there they were, bobbing on the choppy waves of the lake.

"Oh, I see them now."

"So near and yet so far," Tracy said. "I still can't see how three overturned canoes could be washed off the beach and then turn themselves right side up so they sail like little birds, right across the lake."

Ron cast her a grateful look. "That's what I've been thinking. If they'd been washed into the lake upside down, they'd have filled with water if, somehow, they righted themselves. They'd have sunk, not floated the way they're doing."

"It's not too far for me to swim," Tracy said thoughtfully. "Maybe I could swim across the lake and bring back one of the canoes. Then you could paddle out with a rope and tow in the others."

"No way," Ron said. "You'd need a wet suit for something like that. The water's too cold. It's like ice. You'd get hypothermia. Even with a life jacket, it would be suicide."

"You mean we're stuck here in this scummy place for another night?" Melanie asked. "I'll lose my mind!"

Or what's left of it, I thought.

"Then you'd better hang tight," Tracy told her. "There's no telling when the Holmbergs will get here."

Melanie began to sob again. Christabel put her arm around her.

"Take it easy, Melly," she soothed.

I looked out at the lake again. "Why can't we

see any of the life jackets floating around out there? They're bright orange. You'd think they'd show up."

"I've been wondering about that, too," Ron said. "We should be able to spot at least one of them."

"Well, there's nothing we can do here," James said. "We're only getting wet. Wetter," he amended with a wry smile. "I say let's go back to the cabin, dry out, have a cup of coffee, and regroup."

"And unpack while we're at it," Tracy said. "Pack, unpack, pack. I'm starting to feel like a real jet-setter."

"Humph," Christabel said. "Then it sure doesn't take much to give you a thrill."

"Wait a minute," I said. "What's that over there?"

"Where?" James asked.

"There, caught in the roots of that tree!"

I pointed to a huge old pine that was growing along the shoreline beyond where the beach ended. Its massive, intertwined roots had humped up out of the ground and stretched down toward the water's edge.

Something was caught in those roots. Something orange.

"I think I've found one of our missing life jackets," I said.

James jogged over to it and picked it up. He started to return, then stopped and examined the life jacket closely, turning it first one way and then the other.

"Now what?" Christabel asked no one in particular.

"What's up, James?" Ron called.

James returned slowly, still looking at the life jacket.

"What do you think about this?" he said, thrusting the jacket at Ron.

"Maybe a sharp root did it," Ron replied.

"Did what?" I asked.

"Don't bother to ask, Angie," Christabel said snappishly. "They're only doing their big male-bonding thing."

"Did what?" I repeated, ignoring her.

Ron held out the life jacket. "It looks like it's been cut."

"Not cut," James corrected him. "Slashed."

"You don't think a sharp root or a stone could have done it?" Ron asked.

"Hardly. It's been slashed twice—see?—forming a big X."

"So what does that mean?" I asked.

"It means somebody did it. And maybe that same somebody pushed the canoes out into the lake last night."

NINE

"There's someone else on this island!" Ron said. "There has to be. It's the only explanation."

"I think you're right," James agreed, nodding.

I nodded too. "Who else would do that to the canoes and the life jacket?"

We were back at the cabin now, huddled before the fire, drinking hot coffee and trying to get warm.

Ron seemed to be ignoring Christabel's little digs. Having something concrete to worry about was turning him back into his old take-charge self again. He'd lost that hangdog, guilty look.

He wrapped his hands around his coffee mug, warming them. "What I can't figure out, though, is why did he—if there is a "he"—slash that life jacket? It's still usable. Besides, who's going swimming in this weather?"

"I think I know why he did it," I said.

Everyone looked at me.

"He's trying to scare us. He wants us to know he's here, watching us."

"I don't believe this!" Melanie said. "Next, I suppose, you'll be saying he killed Chip."

I didn't answer. I didn't have to. Ron answered for me.

"It's time we stopped tiptoeing around the fact that Chip might really have been murdered."

"Come off it, Ron!" Christabel said. "This is getting more ridiculous by the minute."

He ignored her and addressed the group. "You know the facts. He supposedly slipped and hit his head, but he landed on his face. Not his back, but his *face*. And the rock with the blood on it was a couple of feet from the body, like someone hit him with it and then threw it down. This accidental-death business never made any sense to me."

"Not to me, either," I said. "But—"

James interrupted, finishing my sentence for me. "But since we'd be going home this morning—or so it seemed—there was no point in stirring things up and upsetting everyone any more than they are already. We'd let the police figure out what happened."

He smiled at me apologetically. "Sorry, Angie."

I smiled back. "Be my guest."

I'd noticed that James and I were beginning to function like a team. The way Michael and I had.

"And now it's different?" Tracy asked. "You're saying that we're stuck here, and we'd better face facts and cover our backs?" She winced a little at her accidental poetry.

"That's right," James said.

"Wait a minute! Wait a minute!" Christabel put her hands to her cheeks and shook her head in confusion. "You *really* think there's someone on this island who killed Chip? And that he's the one who fooled with the canoes?"

"Yes."

"You mean, like a crazy hermit or something?"

Christabel had obviously begun to believe us. She was starting to look scared.

"But why would anyone—even a crazy hermit—want to kill Chip?" Melanie asked. Her face was pale beneath her makeup. I noticed the blusher on one cheek was higher than on the other.

"Maybe he just likes to do it," Tracy suggested. "Maybe he's a serial killer. A psychopath."

"And that's why he fixed it so we can't leave," Melanie said slowly and with growing horror. "We're trapped here, and he's going to pick us off one by one!"

"Oh no, he's not!" Ron said. "Not if we find him first."

"So how are we going to do that? Invite him to tea?" Christabel asked sarcastically.

"No, we'll go out and look for him."

"This isn't a big island," I put in, "but if he's been living here, he might know all sorts of hiding places."

"I don't think he's been living here long," James said. "He probably got here only a little ahead of us. Otherwise, don't you think he'd have been living in the cabin?"

He looked at us questioningly. A couple of us nodded in agreement.

"But there was no sign of recent occupancy," he continued. "I had to prime the pump. There weren't any ashes in the fireplace, or blankets in the bedrooms. No food, no dirty dishes. Nothing."

I cleared my throat nervously. "Then how did he get here? There wasn't a canoe on the beach when we arrived."

"That's why we should search the island," Ron said. "He's got to have a canoe stashed somewhere, and it's pretty hard to hide a canoe."

"I'm scared," Christabel said. Her hand fluttered to her throat. "What if he jumps out at us with a knife or something?"

"We'll travel in teams," Ron said. "Tracy and I in one, and James and Angie in the other."

"So where does that leave Melanie and me?" Christabel asked.

"Someone's got to stay in the cabin," Ron insisted. "We don't want him circling back and locking himself in here."

"Are you insane?" Christabel's eyes were wild. "Are you saying Melanie and I are supposed to fight him off if he comes here?"

Ron looked at her. Hard. "I didn't think there was a man in the world you were afraid of, Christabel, or one you couldn't wind around your finger. But just in case, we'll close the shutters. They bolt from inside. He won't be able to get in the windows. And you can put the bar on the door. You'll be safe enough."

"But what if he comes around?"

"I found one of those aerosol boat horns when I sorted out the shed," James said. "I'll get it for you. If he tries to get into the house, just press the lever. We'll be able to hear you no matter where we are."

The shed. Chip was out there. I wondered how James could bear going past his body to get at the shelves. He must have been thinking the same thing, because his face was pale and he'd begun to sweat.

"Would you like me to go with you? Or at least stand in the doorway?" I offered.

He shot me a grateful smile. "Thanks, but I think I can handle it."

"Wait a minute," said Tracy. "Christabel had a point there about him jumping out with a knife. What if he's armed?"

"I won't try to fool you, Tracy," James told her. "We know he's got a knife. He cut the life jacket with it, remember? And if he's got a gun —well, he's going to get us no matter what we do."

"You're not reassuring me, James old buddy," Tracy said.

"I'm betting he doesn't have a gun," Ron said. "If he does, then why didn't he shoot Chip?"

"Maybe Chip scared him and he simply reacted," I said.

Tracy chewed on the side of a fingernail. "Are you *sure* we're doing the right thing? Maybe we shouldn't go out looking for him. Maybe we should just stay here and hole up until the Holmbergs arrive."

"And have him pick them off on the beach? Then we'd definitely be stuck here," Ron said. His jaw was set and resolute. "No, we'll find his hiding place, and then we'll come back here and decide how to put him out of operation. After all, there are six of us and only one of him."

"We hope," Melanie said fervently.

It had stopped raining by the time we started out.

We decided to go around the island in opposite directions. James and I would take the eastern side and head north, Ron and Tracy the western. We'd meet in the middle.

Both search parties started at the beach. Tracy seemed a little reluctant to part and head off in her and Ron's direction. I think she would rather have been James's partner. I didn't blame her.

We left the beach, James and I, and made our way up the wooded coastline.

It was quiet in the woods, except for a funny little bird who kept repeating the same four notes of a song.

James was leading. He stopped suddenly and turned. I bumped into him and found myself in his arms.

"Angie," he said. His voice was low. He said my name again, as if he liked the way it sounded. "Angie. Beautiful Angie."

His arms tightened around my waist, and he pulled me closer. I could feel his heart beating against my chest. It was beating fast, too fast, but so was mine.

I tried to say something. Something light. But I could only smile up at him shakily. I wasn't prepared for this. I wasn't prepared for the way my body was responding to his.

He bent his head to kiss me. I could see the fine line of his eyelashes and the sheen of his eyelids that were closing as he brought his lips down on mine.

And then he kissed me.

His lips felt like warm silk and tasted fresh and spicy.

I could have stayed that way forever, but finally, reluctantly, he stopped kissing me and laid his cheek on my hair. He held me like that for a few moments before he released me.

"I'm sorry," he said, and cleared his throat. "I just had to do that."

I drew a breath. The taste of him still lingered in my mouth, on my lips.

"James . . . ," I said. My voice was fuzzy and indistinct. "James, I can't . . ."

"I know. I'm sorry." He took my elbow and helped me over a rock. I could feel his hand trembling on my elbow. "I had no right to do that. Especially now, with everything else that's been happening. I just couldn't help myself, that's all."

I stopped and looked at him questioningly.

"Don't do that," he commanded. "If you do, I'll only want to kiss you again."

I tried again.

"James," I said. "We shouldn't be doing this. I mean, we shouldn't be starting something this . . . this . . . important. Not now. Not with

Chip murdered and us trapped here on this terrible island."

He put his arm around me and drew me close to him again.

For a moment I weakened and let my body come to rest against his. It was so good to be in his arms and feel loved and protected. But then I made myself take a step backward and push him away.

"Please . . . ," I said.

"I know," he said. "Here I go again, confusing the issue."

He bent his head and stooped slightly, so we were eye to eye. "But when this is over, Angie, I'm not going to let you push me away again. I feel something really special for you, and I think you feel that way about me, too."

When I was younger, I used to imagine scenes like this. But now it was all wrong. I started to say something, but a movement in the trees a few yards away caught my eye.

I clutched James's arm and pulled him behind the nearest tree.

"Look!" I said, pointing. "Over there!"

A gray-haired man in a red flannel shirt and khaki pants slipped from the cover of the woods and hurriedly scrambled down the sandy bank that led to the lake. He disappeared momentarily from our view, but reappeared a few seconds later.

He must have hidden his canoe, since we hadn't spotted it as we'd approached the lakeside turning. But then, we'd been distracted.

We stood stock-still and watched as he pushed the canoe into the water and climbed aboard.

"Did he see us?" I whispered.

"I don't know," James replied. "And if he did, he probably figured we were too busy to stop him."

The man drew an oar from the bottom of the canoe and used it skillfully as he skimmed over the lake, heading out toward the river.

"Did you see that?" James gasped. "The red shirt? And the canoe—it has a blue logo, just like on the ones we rented. It must be the stolen one, remember?"

"Yes," I answered, still whispering. "Which means, he must be Amos, the man who escaped from the mental hospital."

James drew a deep breath.

"So there *was* someone on this island. And now, thank God, he's gone."

He turned to me, and we looked at each other with wide eyes.

"He's gone, Angie, and we're safe!"

Or so it seemed.

TEN

We found Tracy and Ron on the north end of
the island and told them what we'd seen.

Tracy shivered. "So it was that crazy Amos
the whole time! But it's almost too much of a
coincidence, isn't it? With miles of wilderness,
why'd he have to come *here*?"

"Maybe not such a coincidence after all. The
police said he'd grown up on the river, remember?" I told her. "He knew about Shadow Island and the deserted hunting cabin. He
probably figured he could hole up here and no
one would find him."

"But then we came paddling in," James said.
"Three canoes full of noisy high-school kids. He
must have fled into the woods to figure out
what to do next. And then Chip came along and

frightened him. That's when Amos must have picked up the rock and let him have it."

"He probably didn't even mean to kill him," Ron put in. "I guess he felt he was defending himself."

"So why didn't he leave right then?" Tracy asked.

"The storm was coming," James continued. "He knew he couldn't travel on the river with all that wind and rain, so he spent the night hiding out, sheltering as best he could from the storm. And then he got rid of the canoes so we couldn't follow him."

He paused and looked around sheepishly. "Or at least, that's what I *think* happened."

"It makes sense to me," Ron agreed. He rubbed the back of his hand across his eyes. He was always close to tears when he talked about Chip. "I wish Chip hadn't come along and scared him. Or I wish Chip and I had stayed together when we looked for wood. Amos wouldn't have attacked the two of us, and Chip would still be alive."

Tracy reached out and hugged him. "Don't blame yourself, Ron. It wasn't your fault. It simply happened, and there's nothing we can do about it now."

Christabel and Melanie had the cabin locked up tighter than Fort Knox. We had to hammer and shout before they would open up.

When they did, they were clinging together like a pair of Siamese twins. They looked as if they'd been expecting the angel of death.

Their fearful expressions didn't change until we told them about Amos—that it must have been him all along, and how we'd seen him leave the island.

Color flooded back into Christabel's pale cheeks. Her face lost its shrunken, haggard look.

"It's over!" she cried joyfully. "We're safe."

She threw herself at Ron, twining her arms around his neck. He reached up and removed them. Then he pushed her aside.

I was surprised. I didn't know Ron had that much strength of character. There must be a lot more to him, I decided, than meets the eye.

Christabel, beautiful, fascinating Christabel, had thought she could treat him like dirt and then have him come back for more. Well, she was wrong. This must have been a real first in her life.

The cabin was cold. I looked over at the fireplace. She and Melanie had let the fire go out.

Since I seemed to have been unanimously elected Keeper of the Flame, it was up to me, I guessed, to get it going again.

I got down on my knees and began assembling fire starters and kindling.

"Why'd you two let this thing go out?" I grumbled. "It's such a pain getting it started again."

"We didn't want him—the killer—to see smoke coming from the chimney," Christabel explained earnestly. "We didn't want to attract his attention."

"I guess I might as well clean out the ashes while I'm at it," I said. "It's a real mess in there. I'm beginning to see why Cinderella hated her cruel stepsisters."

I reached for the fireplace shovel and began scooping up the ashes and dumping them into the tin bucket that stood on the hearth. There were enough ashes to fill it to the top. I got to my feet and picked up the bucket, groaning at its weight.

"Here, I'll help you, Angie," Tracy volunteered.

Just as she reached out to take the other end of the handle, I dropped the bucket. Ashes flew everywhere, and a gray cloud, like the fallout of a miniature atomic bomb, rose and wafted about the room.

Tracy went into wild fits of sneezing, coming up every now and then for breath. Her eyes ran, and she groped for a tissue. She always had a pack handy.

"Excuse—ah-choo!—me! It's my darned—ah-choo!—allergies!"

I tried to apologize for dropping the ash bucket, but she reached out and fluttered one hand in the air. "Don't worry, I'll be okay in a—ah, ah-choo!—minute."

She finally stopped sneezing and giggled, although her eyes were bleary and her nose running, and gave one last, noisy honk into her tissue.

"Uhhh-ohh," she croaked. "Now I'm all stuffed up."

She disappeared into the bedroom and returned with her blue toiletries bag.

"Thank heaven for modern medicine," she said, rummaging around in the bag and pulling out her nasal spray. The little maroon-and-white bottle was familiar to all of us. She never went anywhere without it.

She inserted the nozzle into first one nostril and then the other, spraying and sniffing.

What happened next occurred almost too quickly to follow.

Suddenly Tracy choked. She gasped for air. Her face turned a dark purplish-red, and her mouth opened and contorted briefly. Then she fell to the floor.

We gathered around her, struck dumb and motionless, staring stupidly, too surprised to react.

"Tracy?" I finally called out. "Tracy?"

I dropped to the floor beside her. "Tracy?"

Her eyes were open and staring, but they weren't moving. Just like Chip's, yesterday. I picked up her wrist. It was limp and flaccid. Was it growing cold already, or was that just my imagination?

I looked up at the others. At first they made no move to help me. Christabel had both fists to her mouth, as if to keep herself from screaming. Melanie's eyes, still red and puffy from crying over Chip, were almost protruding from their sockets.

I've read somewhere that the state of shock is the way the mind protects itself from an unbearable reality. Chip's death yesterday had been an unbearable reality. And now this. Tracy dropping dead before our very eyes. Tracy, who'd always been so healthy and full of life.

"Ron," I said helplessly. "James. Do something. Help me."

James moved first, dropping stiffly to his knees beside me, beside Tracy, like someone emerging from the Twilight Zone. Ron knelt beside Tracy, too, but for some reason—which he probably didn't even understand himself—he began to straighten her spread-eagled legs, arranging them neatly ankle to ankle, as if he could bring her back to life by making her look ladylike.

James felt in vain for Tracy's pulse, first in her wrist and then in her neck. He did something to her eyelids. I think he was trying to see if her eyes would move, but they didn't. So he closed them for her.

Christabel roused herself from her stupor. "What happened?" she said in a whisper.

"Is she . . . is she . . . ?" Melanie stammered.

"Yes," James said. His voice was calm, but his eyes seemed unable to focus on anyone. "Tracy's dead."

ELEVEN

"Dead?" Christabel asked. "Tracy?"

"It's not true!" Melanie shrieked. "No, not Tracy!"

"She was laughing one minute. And then . . ." Ron shook his head and sank down on one of the sagging armchairs that fronted the fireplace.

No one seemed able to cope with what had just happened. Tracy, the fittest of the group. The competitive swimmer. The one with an athletic scholarship waiting for her next year. This was totally unbelievable. Healthy teenagers don't suddenly drop dead.

"Was it a heart attack?" I asked James. I was speaking softly, the way you do in a hushed cathedral.

"There was nothing wrong with Tracy's heart," Christabel put in. Then, in a louder voice, "That girl was as strong as a mule."

James didn't reply. He peered into Tracy's face. Her lips were discolored and twisted.

Tracy's bottle of nasal spray lay on the floor beside her body. James picked it up and cautiously—very cautiously—sniffed at it.

"What are you doing?" I asked.

"Is he playing detective or something?" Melanie said. She was obviously recovering from her initial shock. She directed her next question at James. "And who elected *you* chief inspector?"

"Please, Melanie," I said. "He's only trying to figure out what happened."

"What happened—and it was plain to see what happened—was that she had a heart attack, or some kind of fit," she shot back. "What do we know? We're not doctors. I think we ought to assume it was a heart attack and let the coroners do the rest."

James stood up and wiped his hands on his jeans nervously and compulsively, as if trying to disassociate himself from death.

"We don't have that option, Melanie," he

118

said. "Who knows when help will arrive? In the meantime, we've got to protect ourselves."

"Protect ourselves? From what? You said you saw that crazy Amos—the one who killed Chip —leave the island."

James nodded. "Yes, and I thought we'd be safe. But now this. Tracy. I can't figure it out."

"What do you mean?" I asked.

"Look, you guys, I'm no expert, but I don't think Tracy died a natural death."

Christabel looked briefly at Tracy's body— the discolored face and the outflung arms, one of which still clutched a wad of tissue—and averted her gaze. "It . . . it wasn't a heart attack or a fit?"

"No," James said, shaking his head. "I think there was something in that nasal spray—something Tracy inhaled—that killed her."

"Something? Like what?" Ron asked.

"It has a funny smell. Be careful handling it. If it's what I think it is, it's pretty strong stuff."

"What kind of smell?" I asked.

"Like bitter almonds," he said. "Isn't that the poison they always use in murder mysteries?"

"Cyanide!" I breathed. "You mean cyanide?" I looked down again at Tracy's body.

"Yes, how'd you know?"

"I read a lot of murder mysteries. And my father's a pharmacist, remember?"

"Oh, God," Melanie said. "We've got Sherlock Holmes and Agatha Christie here with us."

Ron rose from his chair. "I wish you'd shut up, Melanie. Can't you get it through your little peanut brain that this isn't one of your soap operas? This is really happening. Two of our friends have been—might have been—murdered."

This was another first for Ron. I'd never heard him talk like that to Melanie. Neither had she, evidently, because she balled her hands in tight fists, and for a wild moment, I thought she might hit him.

James held up his hands. "Wait a minute, everybody. Wait a minute. Let's just calm down. The first thing we have to do is move Tracy . . . Tracy's body . . . out of here. It's not respectful to fight like this around her . . . her remains."

I got Tracy's poncho from the bedroom, and we wrapped her in it. The boys carried her out to the shed. I followed. There were two bodies out there now.

James put his arm around me as we returned to the cabin.

"She had a crush on you, you know," I told him.

"No, I didn't know. She was a great girl. I liked her."

I was silent for a moment. "I did, too." I began to cry. "*Why* did she insist on coming on this trip, James? She didn't have to. If she hadn't, she'd still be alive."

James stopped walking and faced me. He wiped away my tears with his thumbs before he kissed me. And then I felt safe and forgot . . . everything.

When we returned to the cabin, we found Melanie and Christabel on their knees before the cold hearth, trying to start a fire. I knelt beside them and laid the kindling and the fire starters in place and coaxed the new fire along until small flames began to lick at the logs.

Melanie stood before the faintly flickering flames, her teeth chattering. "That shed . . . I couldn't go out there. It's turned into a funeral parlor, hasn't it? It's so cold in here. Is it cold, or is it just me?"

I almost liked Melanie for an instant. That was the first genuine emotion I'd ever heard her express.

She continued to babble. "And now we're supposed to think that Tracy's been murdered, too. Just like Chip. Maybe neither one of them was. Maybe it only looks that way."

"I think it's time we sat down and talked this thing through," Ron said. "We've got to figure out what's happened, and what to do about it."

"I just want to go home," Christabel said. "I wish I'd wake up and find out that this has only been a bad dream."

"I'll fix us some tea," I volunteered. "Strong, with lots of sugar. We need something."

When I'd filled the mugs from the kettle on the hearth, we all came over to the kitchen table and sat down. I noticed everyone had conscientiously avoided stepping on the spot where Tracy had fallen.

Christabel took a sip of her tea, grimacing at its scalding temperature. "This is good," she said, "but I'd give anything for a stiff drink."

She looked over at James. "You don't have your little silver flask with you, James, by any chance?"

I was sitting beside James. He was holding my hand under the table. I felt him give a little start, and his hand suddenly grew cold in mine.

"You know I don't drink anymore, Christabel.

And you know the exact moment I stopped, too, don't you?"

"Really, James!" Christabel said, tossing her head. Her gloriously blond hair flipped over one shoulder. "When are you going to quit acting like a martyr? It was just a party, for God's sakes. What happened wasn't *our* fault."

"I'm glad you can feel that way." James's voice was dry and caustic.

"What are you two talking about?" I asked.

"A stupid drunk, that's what," Christabel said. "This creepy guy got drunk at a party and—"

"He was *tricked* into getting drunk at that party," James said. He wasn't holding my hand anymore. It was clenched, and he was thumping on the table.

"That poor 'creepy guy,' as you call him, was tricked into getting drunk," James said. "And then he . . . he . . . became a traffic statistic on his way home."

"Nice way of phrasing it," Melanie purred. "Is that how your doctor at the funny farm told you to look at it? As a statistic? Did that make you feel better?"

I reached out and grasped Melanie's arm. "Really, Melanie, you shouldn't—"

She shrugged me off. "Oh, come off it, Miss Priss. Do you really expect us to believe you're as sweet and innocent as you pretend to be?"

James's face darkened, and I could see a cheek muscle working, as if he were clenching and unclenching his teeth.

"Leave Angie out of this, Melanie." His voice was low but menacing.

Melanie opened her eyes in mock surprise. "So that's how it is? Sir Galahad and the lily-white maiden. Boy, has she got you fooled, big guy."

She paused a moment, enjoying my confusion. Then she said, "You said you didn't know where James was last semester, Angie. Baloney. Every kid at Oakbridge High knew where he was. Didn't you know that our boy, here, is a regular saint? He likes to feel personally responsible for every jerk he meets."

"That's enough!" Ron snapped from his place at the head of the table. "Leave it alone, Melanie. What's the matter with you? We've got some problems to deal with right now. Real problems. So forget what happened last semester, okay?"

Melanie sank back in her chair, her face sullen.

Christabel turned to Ron. "I really love the way you sum things up." She mimicked him. "'We've got some real problems here, gang.' Well, no kidding, Dick Tracy. Tell us another."

"You don't have to act so damn smart, Chris," Ron said.

"Well, maybe it's time somebody did," she retorted. "We've got two bodies, two dead bodies, out there in the shed. Our friends, for God's sakes. We're supposed to be having a fun week on a deserted island, and we've got two dead friends in a shed. And we're stuck here on this hellhole of an island. And so here we sit, drinking tea, like a bunch of garden-club ladies."

"There's not much else we can do, Christabel," I said.

"Yes, what do you want us to do?" Ron said.

Christabel looked at him, an expression of intense loathing on her beautiful face. "If you were a real man, Ron, like you always pretended to be, none of this would have happened."

"How? How? Tell me how, Chris."

"You tell me, Macho Man. You should have known that Amos would make a beeline for this island."

"That's crazy. How could I have known that?"

"Oh, stop it!" I said. "This is getting us nowhere. And Ron is right, Christabel. He couldn't possibly have known Amos would come to Shadow Island."

"Besides which," James put in, "Amos did not kill Chip."

As if the scene we were acting out had been on stage, and orchestrated for full horror, James's words were punctuated by a bright zigzag of lightning, followed by a clap of thunder.

"Oh no," Melanie moaned. "Not another storm!"

The cabin suddenly grew pitch dark, surrounded by a low wet fog.

"I can't take much more of this!" Christabel snapped.

"This storm is not personally directed against you," Ron said with exaggerated politeness. "It's just one of those puzzling acts of nature."

"Oh, shut up!" Christabel replied.

I reached for the hurricane lamp, which stood in the middle of the table. It had plenty of oil.

"If someone will get me a match, I'll get this

thing going," I said. "My grandmother keeps kerosene lamps in her summer cabin."

"I suppose we're going to have to hear now about your wealthy family and their summer places," Melanie said.

"Stop it!" James was practically shouting. "What's happening to us? We've done nothing but fight ever since we sat down at this table."

"James is right," Ron said. "We're going to pieces. If we're going to survive this thing, we've got to pull together."

"So let's pull together," Christabel said. "God knows, I'd like to survive this weekend. If possible."

"You said Amos didn't kill Chip," Melanie told James. "What are you talking about? You built up quite a case that Amos was a murderer, and then you said you and Angie saw him leave the island in his stolen canoe, and that we were safe at last. So what are you trying to say now?"

James seemed to be trying to organize his thoughts, to get them in order so they would make sense.

"Look," he told us. "The odds against there being *two* murderers on a little island like this are probably a billion to one."

"I don't follow you," Christabel said.

"Look at it this way. If Amos murdered Chip, then who killed Tracy?"

"Amos," Christabel said. "Who else could have done it?"

"How could he? He didn't come anywhere near this cabin. There's been someone here the entire time we've been on the island. And besides, he didn't know Tracy had allergies, or that she kept her spray in that little blue bag near her bed."

"That's right," I agreed.

"But are you sure Tracy was murdered?" Melanie asked.

"Yes," James said. "There was definitely something in that bottle of nasal spray."

Ron's forehead was creased in thought. "So what you're trying to say, James, is that Amos didn't kill Chip. That whoever killed Tracy also killed Chip."

"That's right." James's cheek muscle was at work again.

"But there's no one here on this island but us," Ron said.

"Right."

"No," Ron protested. "What you're saying can't be right."

"Nevertheless," James admitted, "it's true."

The light of the kerosene lantern cast exaggerated shadows on the walls. Our faces looked dark and sinister as we ringed the table. On the mantel, the stuffed owl crouched like an evil demon.

"It's true," James repeated. "Whoever killed Tracy also killed Chip. And that person wasn't Amos. It was one of us."

TWELVE

"One of us?" Christabel echoed. "A murderer?"

Melanie gnawed a long, painted fingernail. She reminded me of a nervous rodent. "Why would anyone—any of us—want to kill Chip?"

"That's the unbelievable part," James said. "You don't murder someone without a reason. A motivation."

Christabel looked sideways at James, a sly, knowing expression on her face. "Some killers don't need any motivation."

"Huh?" Ron said.

"Insane people don't need reasons for what they do." Christabel was looking directly at James now.

James's face reddened angrily, and he started to say something, but she cut him off.

"Let's face it, James. You were acting pretty weird last semester. You could still be weird, but hiding it."

"I suffered from depression last semester, Christabel, not insanity. There's a difference, you know."

I cut in. "Isn't it time that you stopped bringing up the fact that James was under a doctor's care last semester? He's obviously worked out whatever it was that caused his depression."

James flashed me a grateful smile.

I wondered why Christabel kept harping all the time on James's breakdown last semester. He was supposed to be her friend, but so far this trip she had thrown his hospital stay in his face every chance she got. And Melanie—why did she get that secret, pleased expression on her face whenever Christabel did it?

Ron rubbed his face wearily with his hands, making a whiskery, scratchy sound. "I can't figure out what's happening. James is right. You don't kill someone unless you have a good reason."

"Or at least *some* kind of a reason," I said.

"Even an unbelievable one, like those people who kill someone for only a couple of dollars."

"I suppose a case could be made for everyone here, then," James said.

"Not me!" Ron protested. "There's no reason in the world for me to kill Chip or Tracy."

"Okay, Ron. Let's start with you, then," James said. "Remember, now, this isn't an accusation. It's strictly hypothetical."

"So go ahead. Shoot."

"Chip was competing with you for that football scholarship, wasn't he?"

Ron nodded. "Yes, but—"

"And Tracy works—worked—in the principal's office. So maybe she found out that Chip got the scholarship and told you about it. So you killed Chip and then killed Tracy because she would have eventually fingered you as the killer."

"That's a bunch of crap!" Ron yelled. "I sure as hell wouldn't kill my best friend for a lousy scholarship. What do you take me for, anyway?"

Ron half rose from his chair, as though he'd like to go for James's throat.

James raised his hands, palms out, toward Ron. "Take it easy, Ron. I'm not accusing you of anything. I told you this was all pure theory, remember? I'm only trying to show that every one of us here might have had a motive of some kind for murdering Chip and Tracy."

Melanie drank the last of her tea and set the mug on the table, taking great pains to center it on its paper napkin.

"So what about me?" she asked. "Why would I want to kill either of them?"

I was happy to take this one. I held up my hand, as if I were answering a question in English lit class.

James nodded at me. "Okay, Angie. What's your theory about Melanie?"

"Jealousy," I said.

Melanie's eyes narrowed. "Jealousy? I've never been jealous of anyone."

"Let Angie finish," Ron commanded.

"Yes, jealousy," I said. "Chip's been eyeing that new girl in school. What's her name? Oh yes, Tara Michaels. The one with the long red hair and the Barbie-doll figure—"

Melanie snorted.

"Well, anyway, as the poet says, 'Hell hath no fury like a woman scorned,' and you've got a real fiery temper, Melanie."

"Ha, ha! Very funny, Angie. But, for your information, Chip never scorned me. And he took no interest whatever in that little tramp, Tara Michaels. So tell me, why would I kill Tracy?"

"Probably for the same reason. Jealousy," I said. "Didn't Tracy just beat you out for head cheerleader for football season next year? I hear you had your heart set on it. You're not one to take defeat easily, Melanie. And besides, being named head cheerleader would have given you a lot of status in Chip's eyes. Maybe even made him forget Tara Michaels."

If Melanie hadn't been sitting across the table from me, I'm sure she would have scratched my face with those long, clawlike nails of hers.

Instead, she said, "You've got a big mouth, Angie. And you're shooting it off to hide the fact that you've got more reasons for killing Chip and Tracy than I do. Did. Whatever."

"Reasons? Like what?"

"Like you had a mad crush on Chip and he never paid any attention to you. So you got mad and killed him. Maybe you tried to come on to him out there in the woods, and he rejected you."

I was almost speechless with astonishment.

"Me? A crush on Chip? I have never, *never* been attracted to Chip, Melanie. He wasn't my type. Not to speak ill of the dead, but he was a real meathead."

"Oh yeah? Chip was the biggest hunk at Oakbridge High. I saw the way you used to look at him."

"I did not!"

"But he never even looked at you, did he? I was the one he couldn't keep his hands off of."

I was tempted to tell Melanie she had just ended a sentence with a preposition, but wisely refrained.

"So why did I kill Tracy, then?" I asked calmly.

"Maybe she knew you killed Chip and you wanted to shut her up."

"But she didn't say anything? She had all that time to tell on me, but didn't. Why not?"

Melanie appeared flustered. I knew I had her on that one.

"I don't know," she finally admitted. "I haven't had much experience in figuring out who might be killing my friends. But I will say this, Angie—"

She leaned forward across the table. She drew her red lips together in a thin line. "If anyone here on this camping trip could pull off a murder, it's you!"

"How dare you say something like that!" I said. "And how do you justify your accusation?"

"You're cold, Angie. Inside. Oh, sure, you act all sweet and friendly, but I've seen you carve up a frog in biology lab."

I burst into wild laughter. I couldn't help myself. "You think I'm a murderer because it doesn't bother me to dissect a frog in biology?"

"Well . . . yes."

"Look, Melanie, I'm interested in science. I might even go premed in college. I couldn't if I vomited every time I had to look at a dead frog or earthworm, could I? So what do you think Dr. Albert Schweitzer was, a mass murderer?"

She looked embarrassed, but made one more pathetic stab at humiliating me.

"No, but Dr. Hyde in that story was."

"Wrong again, Melanie. He was *Mr.* Hyde. And *Dr.* Jekyll was the good guy."

Melanie's response was typical of her. "Oh, go to hell, Angie!"

"Okay, cut it out," Ron said. "Fighting won't get us anywhere."

Christabel ran her fingers slowly through her long silken hair and asked, "So what about me? Why would I want to kill Chip and Tracy? Does

137

anyone here think I'm jealous? Of anybody? Or anything?"

"No, not jealous," Ron said. "Your ego is too massive for that. I'd say you come under the insanity theory, Christabel. You know, that crazy people don't need any reason to do what they do."

Christabel stopped caressing her hair and looked daggers at Ron.

Watching Ron and Christabel glare angrily at each other over the table reminded me of something I'd read once—that hate was the reverse side of the coin called love. We were definitely seeing that side of the coin now. If looks could kill, Ron would be out in that cold shed along with Chip and Tracy.

James broke the tension.

"Maybe this wasn't such a good idea after all. It certainly isn't getting us anywhere. Besides, all our theories sound pretty lame. No one seems to have an acceptable motive for killing Chip and Tracy."

"Well, *I* don't, that's for sure," Melanie said.

"What should we do, then?" I asked, pointedly ignoring Melanie. "What *can* we do until help arrives?"

James peered at his watch. "Let's see. It's

just a little past three. The earliest the Holmbergs can get here, I'd guess, is around two o'clock tomorrow afternoon."

"That's right," Ron said. "The shape they were in yesterday morning, they'll probably need two days to recover."

"Okay," I said. "So they had yesterday and today to get well. And they'll probably leave tomorrow morning, then, right after breakfast?"

"Right," Ron said. "Which means they ought to reach Shadow Island at the same time we did yesterday."

Melanie's voice was shrill. "Yesterday? Has it been only twenty-four hours since we landed on this godforsaken island? It seems like *years*!"

"Time goes by fast when you're having a good time," I couldn't resist saying.

She rewarded me with a scowl.

"You didn't answer Angie's question, James," Christabel said. "She asked what we should do between now and the time the Holmbergs arrive."

James glanced over at the door. The storm was lessening. The thunder seemed to be moving off, and the rain was letting up. At least for now.

"There's not much we *can* do. I'm afraid

we're pretty much stuck here in this cabin, Chris. Even if the weather clears, the woods are going to be wet. But maybe it's better we all stay here, in the cabin, together. If we stay close and keep our eyes on each other, we're bound to be safe."

"You think, then," Ron said, "that there could be more . . . murders?"

"Who knows?" James replied.

"I simply can't accept the idea that the murderer could be one of *us*," I said.

"There must be another explanation for all this," Christabel said. "Granted there are some real pigs in this group"—she glanced meaningfully at Ron—"but no one I'd consider *murderous*."

"I'm with you, Chris," Melanie said. "I'll bet the police say Chip really *did* hit his head on a rock and that Tracy had a heart attack or something. That business about the bitter almond smell in the nasal spray sounds like someone's been reading too many murder mysteries."

"I hope you're right," I said.

"In the meantime, another twenty-four hours in this rat hole is going to send me over the top," Melanie said, getting up from her chair. "This sitting around is driving me crazy."

"I brought a couple of books with me," I said. "You're welcome to them."

"Oh, yeah? What are they about, the history of electricity and all you wanted to know about the bubonic plague but were afraid to ask?"

"No. Actually, one is *The Great Gatsby* and the other is *The Grapes of Wrath*. We're supposed to read them for English lit."

"Give me a break," Melanie groaned. "*The Grapes of Wrath*! Fun, fun."

"Maybe James brought some more tapes of the Oakbridge High orchestra?" Christabel put in snidely.

"As a matter of fact, I did," James said. "I taped their entire production of *West Side Story*."

Even I had to groan at that.

We all rose and followed Melanie into the living room. There was nothing much to do but move from room to room and chair to chair.

I couldn't help thinking how we all seemed to want to keep busy doing common, ordinary things like sitting before the fire and listening to music. Anything—anything—to keep from thinking about the two bodies in the shed and what might have killed them.

141

Ron sat thinking, absentmindedly rubbing an unshaven cheek.

"We've got a flare gun," he announced suddenly.

"A flare gun? Wasn't it in the canoe?" I asked.

"No. It was in the gear I brought up to the cabin."

"So we've got a flare gun," Christabel said. "So what?"

"We could shoot it off. Maybe someone would see."

"I doubt it, Ron. Not in this weather," James said. "Besides, we're a long way from anywhere."

I looked over at the fireplace. "I hate to say this, but we need more firewood."

"Why? The basket's nearly full," Melanie said.

"But it won't last until tomorrow afternoon," I explained. "And the wood will be wet. We've got to bring it in now so it can dry. Besides, it might start to storm again."

"Well, I'm not staying in this creepy old cabin this time," Christabel said.

"Me neither," Melanie said. "Last time, I had

to go clean the outhouse. *This* time, you can bet I'm on the wood-gathering detail."

"I'll stay," I said. "We haven't eaten anything all day. I'll fix something while the rest of you bring in the wood."

James put his hands on my shoulders and touched his cheek, briefly, to mine. "Are you sure you'll be okay here by yourself?"

I smiled into his eyes. "Yes. I'll lock up, and besides, I have that boat horn to blast if I need help."

"Oh, how very sweet," Melanie snickered. "Young lovers being gallant in the face of danger."

James only shook his head and rolled his eyes.

Everyone donned ponchos and rain hats and set out into the woods. Melanie and Christabel carried plastic bags, as Tracy and I had yesterday, for the twigs and small lengths of wood we would need for kindling. James and Ron went off together for the bigger logs.

A short while after everyone had left, Ron appeared at the door.

I opened it for him.

"Hey, Angie, how come this thing's not locked?"

"I must have forgotten."

"That's pretty dumb, isn't it, with everything that's been happening?"

"Yes. I won't do it again. But why are you here, anyway?"

Ron went to the corner of the living room and began rummaging in one of the boxes. "I've come for that flare gun."

"So you and James are going to set it off after all? Is that what you've decided?"

"No. It's what *I've* decided. James doesn't know I've come back for it. I told him I had to use the outhouse. He'll see I was right when help arrives because they've seen the flare."

I had a sense of déjà vu when the wood gatherers returned to the cabin—that same smell of wet pine had clung to the air when we'd brought in the wood yesterday. The same dripping ponchos. The same thumping of logs as James piled them in the corner by the hearth.

And, just like yesterday, someone was missing.

Ron. Ron was missing.

THIRTEEN

"Where's Ron?" James asked, looking around.

I laid a plate of sandwiches on the trestle table. "You mean he didn't find you after he shot off the flare?"

"Flare?"

"Yes, he came back to the cabin for the flare gun. Said he was going to surprise you by sending up a flare and getting help."

"When was this?"

"A little while after you left. Why?"

"I thought that was what he was up to. He told me he had to use the outhouse. I waited and waited, but he never came back. I did hear a popping noise from down on the beach, though."

He paused and a look of concern came over his features. "He should be back by now."

"Maybe he's waiting to see if anyone's responding to the flare," I suggested.

James was shrugging himself back into his poncho. "I'd better check it out."

I tucked some plastic wrap around the sandwiches to keep them from getting stale. "Wait, James. I'll go with you."

"Now what's wrong?" Christabel asked, rising up from the depths of the sagging old sofa, where she'd flung herself in a pose of melodramatic exhaustion.

"It's Ron," I answered. "He hasn't come back. We're going down to the beach to see if he's there."

"Maybe he's decided to try to walk on water," she said. "He'd do anything to get out of here."

She stood up and fluffed her hair, wiggling her fingers through it and then throwing it back. "I guess I'd better come, too. He's probably up to something stupid."

"Wait for me!" Melanie squawked. "I'm not staying here alone!"

* * *

We made our way down the rocky path to the beach. The sky was a dark gray—the shade you always associate with funerals. Why does it always rain at funerals? I wondered. Or *does* it? Maybe you remember them that way even if the sun shines. Well, I thought, when I remember this week, the rain won't be imaginary. In the future, whenever it rained, I would think of Shadow Island. And death.

The storm had moved off, but the rain continued, a stubborn little afterthought of drizzle. I could see the black clouds that had held the thunder and lightning drifting slowly off over the lake, as if searching for a new spot of land to torment. Then I saw the tall pine trees on the other side of the lake begin to bend and writhe in preparation for the storm.

That's not all I saw.

I saw something on the beach. Something terrible.

Christabel saw it the very same instant I did. She reached out and dug her long fingernails into my arm. "Oh my God, it's Ron!"

Melanie, who was following close behind, slammed up against us. Her eyes widened with horror when she saw Ron—or what used to be

Ron—lying face downward on the sand by the water's edge.

We walked forward slowly, dragging our feet. Melanie and Christabel were hanging on to me like two giant, clinging leeches.

It was like seeing Chip all over again, only this time it was worse. Much worse. The back of Chip's head had been covered with blood, but the back of Ron's was missing, as though it had been blown away, leaving only a mass of bloody pulp.

"His head!" Christabel said in a high, tight voice. "It's gone!"

She repeated the words several times, as if the condition of the body, not the fact that Ron obviously was dead, was the most important thing about the terrible scene before them.

James had sprinted on ahead and was bending over the body.

"Don't come any closer, girls," he said in a strange, strangled voice. Then he leaned over and was violently sick on the sand.

That seemed to set Melanie off, too. She began to make moaning, wailing sounds.

Christabel sat down on the sand, hard, with a plop, as if someone had pulled her long legs out from under her.

I pried Melanie's fingers loose from my arm and ran over to James. His eyes were bloodshot from the convulsive dry heaves he was now having.

He finally stopped heaving and went to the lake, scooping water into his mouth, rinsing and spitting.

I silently offered him a handful of tissue, averting my eyes from Ron's body.

"How did it happen?" I asked quietly.

He wiped his mouth and pointed. "He was shot with the flare gun."

The flare gun, looking like a plumped-up pistol, lay on the sand a few feet away from the body.

"And this was no accident, Angie," he said. "This time there's no question about it. It was murder. Ron was shot in the back of the head. The *back* of the head. Someone else had to do it."

Melanie and Christabel were close enough to hear what we were saying.

Christabel pulled herself shakily to her feet and stood there swaying, not coming any closer to the body.

"His head isn't there! The back of his head's

149

gone!" she said again. "Can't you do something? Cover it up or turn him over or something?"

"What are we going to do with the body?" I asked.

James stripped off his poncho. "I'm going to cover him up and leave him right here. There's no way we can carry him up the hill to the shed. You and I can't do it alone, and those two would be no help."

Christabel took a step backward, dragging Melanie with her. "Oh no, please! I just couldn't. I couldn't touch him."

James dragged Ron's body away from the water's edge—far enough so that it couldn't be washed away in case of a storm. Then he gently turned Ron over.

Ron's face was undamaged, untouched. His mouth was a little open, though, as if he'd started to scream, but was interrupted by death. James covered Ron's head with the poncho, drawing it over his body and weighing down the edges with some large rocks.

I picked up the flare gun gingerly, holding it out at arm's length. "I guess we'd better take this back with us. We'll have to show it to the police, won't we?"

"You shouldn't have picked it up that way,

Angie," James said, looking up. "Now your fingerprints are all over it."

The sight of me holding the flare gun seemed to unhinge Christabel.

"Is it loaded?" she asked in a high, trembling voice.

"No. It only holds one charge at a time," I assured her. "It's empty."

Christabel looked around distractedly. "There are only four of us now."

Christabel and Melanie stood together on the sand, their arms around each other.

James got to his feet and started to come over to her and Melanie, but the girls hastily backed away.

"There are only four of us now," Christabel repeated. "And Ron was murdered. That means one of us—one of us four—is a killer."

James and I exchanged glances. His face was grim, and his lips were pressed tightly together. There were little grayish-white shadows around his eyes. I must have looked as bad as he did, because he came to me and put his arm around my shoulder, pulling me to him.

"Yes," he said. "One of us is a killer, Christabel. There's no question about that now."

"Well, it wasn't me," Christabel said. "And it wasn't Melanie. So it has to be one of you!"

She pointed with a trembling finger at James and me. "Maybe it's both of you. Yes, that's it. It's the two of you. It's a conspiracy. You two got together and decided to kill the rest of us!"

"You're wrong," I said. "Or you're pretending. You're a good actress, Christabel. That's why you always get the lead in every school production. Maybe it's *you*. Maybe *you're* the killer!"

"Or Melanie," James said. "Why couldn't it be Melanie? Did the two of you split up in the woods, or did you stick together every minute?"

"No, we didn't," Melanie answered. "Stick together every minute, I mean. I had to go to the bathroom, but I didn't want to use that awful outhouse. So I went off in the woods, far enough away so no one could see me."

"You were gone a long time, Melanie," Christabel said, narrowing her eyes.

"And you weren't there when I came back," Melanie accused. "Where were you, Chris?"

"On my way to the cabin, carrying my bag of kindling *and* yours, since you weren't anywhere around."

"That's what you say," I told her. "But you

could have been down at the beach, couldn't you, Christabel? Or maybe it was the other way around. Maybe Melanie was down there. Either one of you could have killed Ron, although it's more likely *you* did it."

She made an angry move toward me, and I shrank back. James tightened his arm around my shoulder. I could feel him trembling.

"Why? Why me?" Christabel demanded. "What makes you think *I* killed Ron?" she demanded.

"Because he was shot in the back," I said. "A person turns his back on people for two reasons. First, because he trusts them and isn't afraid he's going to be attacked by them. Or second, he's angry at them and turns his back as a way of telling them to bug off. You could fall into either category, Christabel."

"That's not true!"

"Maybe you went down to the beach to try for a reconciliation and he rejected you, so you picked up the flare gun and shot him."

"Liar! You're lying!"

"What about you, Angie?" Melanie demanded. "Weren't you alone in the cabin? Maybe you followed Ron down to the beach

153

and shot him. And what about James? Didn't he say he was alone in the woods?"

"Why? Why would I shoot Ron? Why would James?"

"How should I know? But someone's killing our friends, and I'm sure not going to turn my back on either you or your clever, know-it-all boyfriend."

"Don't say any more, Melanie," Christabel cautioned. "Can't you see we're unprotected here on the beach? Whoever's doing the killing is crazy. Come on!"

She grabbed Melanie by the arm and half dragged her across the sand.

"Where are you going? Stop!" James called after them.

"Hurry, Melanie!" Christabel urged.

"They're hysterical," James said.

"Either that or Chris is trying to get Melanie alone. Do you think she's the killer?"

"I don't know, but we can't take the chance," he replied, running off behind them. I followed as quickly as I could.

"Oh God, Chris!" Melanie shrilled. "They're chasing us!"

The two girls scrambled up the path to the cabin and took the stairs two at a time. James and I had just reached the porch when the door slammed in our faces. We heard the bolt slam into place.

We were locked out.

Melanie and Christabel had locked me out with James.

FOURTEEN

I hammered on the door. "Let us in!"

"Never!" Melanie screamed.

"You only want to get in so you can kill us," Christabel yelled.

"Don't be silly," James said. "Angie and I can't stay out here all night. It might rain again."

"Then go sleep in the shed," Christabel called. "You're the ones who killed the others. Go stay with them."

I put my mouth up close to the door and said as calmly as possible, "Listen to me. Both of you. Can you hear me?"

I heard a little babble of assent from the other side of the door.

"We don't know who's been doing the killing.

Our only chance of survival is to stick together —all four of us," I said.

"Our only chance of survival is to keep away from you two!" Christabel called back through the door.

"How do you know, Chris? How do you know that Melanie isn't the killer? She has more reasons for killing the others than either James or I do. And maybe she has you pegged as her next victim."

Silence on the other side of the door.

"Melanie," I went on. "How do you know it wasn't Chris? She was the one angry with Ron. And she's the one who dragged you up to the cabin and locked the two of you in together. Maybe she wants to be alone with you so she can kill you, too. Maybe she's a homicidal maniac!"

There was another beat, maybe two, of silence. Then I heard the sound of a bolt being slowly and reluctantly slid open.

The door opened a crack. I could see Melanie's eye peering at me.

"Are you sure that flare gun's not loaded?"

"Absolutely," I assured her. "The other charge is in the box in the corner."

The eye disappeared.

"Do you think we should let them in, Christabel?" I heard her ask.

"Oh, hell, why not?" Christabel's voice was full of bravado. "If we all stick together, we ought to be okay. It's only when we split up that something happens."

The door swung open, and James and I were allowed to enter.

"Thank you very much," I said with exaggerated politeness.

I took off my poncho, shook it out, and hung it on a peg by the door. Melanie and Christabel followed suit.

Then I went over to the fire and threw on another log.

"Am I the only person with the necessary intelligence to see when the fire's burning low?" I snapped.

I didn't wait for an answer, but went into the bedroom and changed into dry clothes.

I didn't hear a sound from the living room as I dressed. I wondered what the girls were up to. They had certainly banded together, those two. But then, they'd been sticking together like glue from the very beginning of the trip.

When I came back to the living area, Melanie

and Christabel were huddled before the fire, drying themselves out.

"Why didn't you come change?" I asked them. "Were you afraid I might attack you with a lethal weapon, like a sharp zipper or something?"

"I'm . . . I'm all right," Christabel said. "I'll be dry in a minute."

James came out of his bedroom, toweling his wet hair. He'd changed into dry jeans and a sweatshirt.

"My stomach's empty," he said with a wry smile. "All that business on the beach. I can't believe it, but I'm hungry now."

I gestured toward the table. "I made sandwiches earlier."

"Sounds good," he said.

"Not me," Christabel said, looking at the sandwiches suspiciously. "I want to make my own."

"So do I," said Melanie.

"Suit yourself. The peanut butter's on the sink," I told them. "What about something to drink? Would you like a cup of tea?"

"I'll get my own mug and put in my own tea bag, thank you," Christabel said stiffly.

"Me too," said her faithful little echo.

I filled the teakettle at the sink, pumping with one hand and holding the kettle with the other. Then I put the kettle on the spider and snuggled it into the fire.

James came up to me as I bent over the fire. He put his arm around me.

"Maybe we made a mistake, insisting they let us in," I said in a low voice. "Maybe it's dangerous, being penned up with them like this."

James glanced over his shoulder. The two girls were in the eating area, making sandwiches. They couldn't hear what was being said.

"What choice did we have?" he asked. "Where else could we go?"

"I know," I said wearily. "I just wanted you to reassure me."

I straightened, putting my hand on his encircling arm, holding it—his warmth—against me for a moment.

"If we can only make it through the night, James. Please stay with me. Every moment. I feel safe when you're close to me."

"I will," he promised. "And . . . and thank you, Angie."

"For what?"

"For not thinking I'm the one. The killer."

"Why should I? You don't suspect me, do you?"

"Of course not. You're too gentle and balanced. I guess that's what attracted me to you in the beginning. You seemed so calm and, well, *together*."

Strange. That's just what Michael used to tell me.

I hastily pushed that thought away. Would I never stop remembering Michael?

"It's got to be one of them," James said. "But which? They're both acting as if they're scared to death."

"Christabel's a real actress," I pointed out. "And Melanie's a fake. Neither one of them ever tells the truth. About anything."

Christabel came up and put her blue enameled mug down on the hearth for me to fill when the kettle boiled. Melanie did, too. It looked almost friendly—four little blue mugs sitting in a row, with the strings of the tea bags hanging out like small tails.

"What time is it?" Christabel asked.

"Nearly five o'clock," I told her.

"Only five o'clock? It seems much later."

It did seem much later. The drizzling rain

and overcast skies, the high surrounding woods, made the cabin dark and gloomy.

There was another kerosene lamp on the mantelpiece. It was full. If anything, the cabin was certainly well prepared for storms and darkness.

I lighted it. I'd hoped the lamplight would be cheering. Instead it only made things eerier. It magnified our shadows as they moved on the walls and did strange, sinister things to the lines and angles of our faces.

Sitting there before the fire, waiting for the kettle to boil, a fragment of a psalm came to me from some remote chamber of my memory. Something about "those who sit in darkness and the shadow of death . . ." That's all I could remember of it, but it was apt. We four sat in darkness and the shadow of death.

I laid out the sandwiches I'd made that afternoon for James and me. Christabel and Melanie brought their own to eat before the warmth of the fire. James ate hungrily. The rest of us merely picked at the food.

Mainly we all watched each other. There was no sense in trying to disguise it now. There were four of us sitting before the fire, and one was a murderer. "Who is it?" each of us seemed to be asking. "Is it you?"

And, "Will there be another murder? Will I be the victim this time?"

I'll never eat peanut butter again, I thought. It will always remind me of this moment.

I looked at the others. They were all chewing now, cowlike, on their sandwiches. It was hardly a scene from one of Agatha Christie's novels, I thought. Her victims always drank sherry and ate crumpets.

Maybe Christabel was thinking of Agatha Christie, too, because she suddenly stopped chewing and cried, "The cyanide!"

We all stopped, hands halfway to our mouths, as if we were playing that childhood game of statues, where you must freeze in midmotion.

"Cyanide?" James echoed apprehensively. Obviously he thought she was trying to tell us she'd been poisoned. "Are you all right, Christabel?"

"Of course I'm all right," she responded impatiently. "But I just thought of something. If Tracy was killed by cyanide, wouldn't the murderer have a bottle of it somewhere in his—or her—belongings?"

"But what if he—or she—used it all?" Melanie asked.

"Then the murderer probably threw the bottle away in the woods somewhere," I said.

"But maybe it's still here, in the cabin," Christabel said. "And maybe if we searched everyone's stuff, we can find it. And then we'll know who the murderer is."

James and I exchanged glances. He shrugged. "It might be a good idea. Let's do it."

We finished eating and drained our mugs.

"Should we start in my room?" James asked.

He stood by, his arms folded across his chest as we went through his things. He hadn't brought much. Just jeans and sweats and some clean underwear. There was only one bottle in his shaving kit, and it was unmistakably aftershave. No sign of cyanide here.

Melanie's cosmetic case was another story altogether. It was filled with little travel-size bottles, each meticulously labeled. There were bottles of toners and moisturizers, plus a rack of bottles offering a whole palette of coloring agents: foundation, highlighter, blusher, and eye shadow.

It took quite a bit of time to cautiously sniff our way through them, but again, no cyanide.

Christabel hadn't brought as many cosmetics as Melanie, but it was still a formidable collection. Then, as we had with the others, we went through her clothing and shoes. No little surprise bottles among her belongings. Well, of course not. She wouldn't have suggested a search if there had been.

I was a little embarrassed when Melanie pawed through my clothes. I was sure she made a point of holding up my underwear in order to humiliate me in front of James. It's not that I'm modest. It's just that they looked so raggedy. Buying new underwear has always seemed like a waste of time and money to me, since no one ever sees them.

Well, they were certainly on display now. I would have preferred them to look like something from "Victoria's Secret," but what the heck.

No cyanide. Naturally. Even though Christabel stuck her hand down in the toes of my hiking boots and spare sneakers and felt all around. She and Melanie gave my things a particularly thorough going-over, obviously trying to communicate that they thought, or would have liked to think, I was The One.

"So what do we do now?" I asked when the

search had ended. "Are you satisfied, Christabel, that neither James nor I plans to poison your toothpaste tonight?"

"Don't be such a smart ass, Angie," she retorted. "Maybe we didn't find any cyanide in your stuff, but you're not in the clear yet."

We all decided, for safety's sake, to sleep together in the living area. Besides, it would be warmer that way, sleeping in front of the fire. The night had turned bitter cold.

We brought in our sleeping bags and laid them out, each at a distance from the other. Then I topped up the fire, and we carried in more logs from the porch. It was agreed that, even when we went to bed, we'd leave a kerosene lamp burning on the trestle table. That and the fire in the fireplace would keep the room well lit all night.

Making it through the night seemed to be on everyone's mind. Make it through the night. Then make it through the morning. And then the Holmbergs will come and take us out of this terrible place. The trick was to stay together. The four of us. In full view of each other every moment.

We even went, all together, out to the little house at the edge of the woods.

"I'll have to share your flashlight, James," I said. "Mine doesn't seem to be working."

"Would you like me to take a look at it?" he asked. "Maybe I can fix it."

"No, never mind," I said. "It's old and I've packed it away. I'll borrow yours if I need to go out again during the night."

He looked horrified. "If you need to go out again in the night, wake me up. Promise?"

"I promise," I told him. "I wouldn't want to go anywhere by myself."

We walked back to the cabin, the four of us, all in a line, like baby chicks following a mother hen, following the gentle shine of the kerosene lamp I'd placed in the window of the cabin to guide us home.

There was no sign of rain now, not even the gentle, drizzling mist we'd been having. The stars had come out, and we could see them shining down through the trees. They looked so far away, so far removed from what was going on here, down below. Lucky stars.

We went to bed early. There was no sense in sitting there, staring at each other and looking frightened. Even if we couldn't sleep, at least we could lie there in our sleeping bags and have some private time to think.

I heard them drop off, one by one. I heard James's breathing grow deep and regular. Then Melanie, making occasional honking noises, and Christabel, who snored. She would be mortified, I thought, if she knew.

Finally I fell asleep, too. It was a restless sleep; I dreamed of monsters and dead bodies. In one of the dreams Ron was looking in the window at me. Ron, with his head the way it had been on the beach when we found him.

He was levitating up and down before the window, the way I'd once seen a vampire in an old movie do. The vampire hung in the air, moving slowly up and down, rapping on the window and begging the woman inside to let him in. That's how it is with vampires, you know, if you've ever seen any of those movies. They can't come in unless the victim invites them.

And that was what Ron was doing. Asking me to let him in.

"Please, Angie, let me innnnn," he moaned, turning his head so I could see the full horror of his injury. "Let me innnnn!"

I woke up, gasping, my heart beating a mile a minute.

The others were still sleeping. I evidently hadn't made any noise.

I looked over at the window. Nothing there, thank God. For a moment I had feared I might still see Ron, framed in the outer darkness.

I waited until my pulse stopped racing and then rolled over quietly in my sleeping bag and went back to sleep.

But just as I was dropping off, a strange, niggling thought crossed my mind. One I was too tired to pursue.

Why hadn't James thought of looking for the cyanide? He always thought of everything. Right after Tracy died, why hadn't he suggested we search for the cyanide?

FIFTEEN

Sunlight, bright sunlight, shining in through the window awakened me the next morning. For a moment, I almost forgot where I was.

Then it all came back.

Bodies were stirring in the other three sleeping bags. Someone coughed.

I unzipped my bag and crawled out. No need to dress, as I had slept in jeans and a sweatshirt. Everyone had. We all wanted to be dressed and ready in case of an . . . emergency.

Again, as we had the night before, we walked in a single column, all together, to the rickety little outhouse at the edge of the woods.

"Listen," I told James as we walked slowly back to the cabin, "I can hear birds."

Although Christabel and Melanie were now

speaking to James and me only when absolutely necessary, they stopped, too, and listened to the cheerful chirping sounds of the birds.

"I guess they've been hiding out from all the rain we had," James said.

"It sounds almost . . . normal," Christabel said, unbending a little.

"Normal!" Melanie said with a strained laugh. "That must be the most beautiful word in the dictionary."

We all nearly smiled at each other. It was that kind of morning. The terrible events of the past two days almost seemed like a bad dream, nothing more.

But then I glanced down at the beach as we passed an opening in the trees. I stopped and shuddered, remembering last night's dream where Ron was at the window, begging me to let him in.

It was only a dream, I told myself. Ron is down there, shattered and dead, weighted down by a poncho and a few rocks.

"Oh God, poor Ron," Christabel said, following my gaze.

I suddenly thought of something.

"James," I said, "will Ron be the first thing

the Holmbergs see when they beach their canoe? I mean, that'll be quite a shock, won't it?"

"I doubt they'll realize it's a body. It's well covered. We'll break the news to them as gently as possible when we get them to the cabin."

"Good!" Melanie said. "I wouldn't want them to panic and paddle off."

Breakfast was as sparse as supper had been the night before.

I rifled through the food box and came up with some fresh fruit and a couple of boxes of Pop-Tarts. We also had a large number of canned things and dehydrated meals, but Christabel and Melanie vetoed those since that would require a certain amount of preparation.

"The less handling of food the better," Christabel said. "We've had one poisoning. We don't want another."

"But none of us have any poison in our stuff," I told her. "We searched last night, remember?"

Christabel pressed her lips together in a thin line. "Better to be safe. The Pop-Tarts are in sealed packages."

"Does anyone want coffee?" I asked. "Personally, I'm sticking to herb tea. I'm too nervous right now for any caffeine."

"You're probably right." James looked at the others inquiringly. "Is tea okay with you?"

"Sure," Melanie said. "I'm jumpy enough as it is."

I filled the kettle and set it on the iron spider, pushing it in against the flames of the newly rekindled fire. The others rinsed out their blue enameled mugs, added tea bags, and set the mugs on the hearth, just as they had the night before.

I lingered on in the kitchen, straightening up the food box and wiping out the sink.

"The water's boiling," James called from the living room. "Bring your cup, Angie, and I'll pour."

"No, I'll do the honors," I said wearily. "The handle on that teakettle is tricky. It's about to come off."

I laid my mug on the hearth, with the others, and, using a hot pad, gingerly plucked the kettle from the flames.

Then I filled the mugs and handed them out.

"That one's not mine," Christabel said. "It's Melanie's. Mine's the one on the end."

"Sorry," I said. "Is this yours, Melanie? It was second from the right."

Melanie snatched it rather ungraciously from

my hand. "Yes. I'm going to write my name on my cup next time."

"Maybe next time you can take care of the fire and heating the kettle, too," I snapped.

We didn't bother to sit at the trestle table, but remained where we were, in front of the fire.

Christabel examined her Pop-Tart package carefully for possible tampering. Apparently satisfied, she tore it open with her long finger-nails.

She bit a delicate crescent from the pastry. "Maybe we're concentrating too much on the possibility of poisoning," she said. "Ron was shot with the flare gun. It's still around here somewhere. What did you do with it, James?"

James looked up, surprised. "You're right, Chris. I hadn't thought about that. I should have, I know, but seeing Ron . . . like that . . . kind of wiped me out. I wrapped the gun in a towel and laid it on Ron's bunk. But at least I remembered to put it away for evidence."

"Oh, James," I said. "My fingerprints are all over that gun. The police won't think I did it, will they?"

"The murderer's prints ought to be on it, too, Angie."

"But what if the murderer wore gloves? Then it will only be *my* prints on the gun."

"I wouldn't worry about it too much," he said. "All of us here can attest to the fact that we saw you carry it up from the beach."

Melanie, who'd been sitting moodily quiet in her armchair, not eating, suddenly began to laugh.

"Yeah, don't worry, Angie," she said. "We'll all swear it wasn't you. We'll tell them the butler did it. Isn't that the one who always does it in the movies?"

"What's the matter with you, Melanie?" Christabel stared at her. "Are you okay or what? What's this butler stuff?"

Melanie shrugged. "Who else can it be? Everyone here says they're innocent. So if we're all innocent, who did it? Who killed Chip? And Tracy? And Ron? Did you see his head? It looked like a pot of stewed raspberries."

"Please, Melanie," I said. "Please don't talk about that now."

She laughed again. Her laughter had a frightening, hysterical quality to it.

We all looked apprehensively at her. She'd acted all right earlier this morning. What was happening to her now?

She seemed to sense what we were thinking.

"Oh, stop looking at me like that! I'm only playing detective."

She laughed again. "Maybe it wasn't the butler. Maybe the ghost did it."

She glanced around at our blank faces.

"The ghost. Remember? Someone said the cabin was haunted. It was Tracy. That's who it was. Tracy said the cabin was haunted. So maybe the ghost killed her so she wouldn't tell on him."

This time her laughter was uncontrollable.

I did what I'd always read about in books. I leapt up from my chair, went over to her, and gave her a stinging slap, first on one cheek and then on the other.

It worked. I'd always wondered about that.

Melanie abruptly stopped laughing and looked stunned. Then she began to cry.

Christabel was at her side in a moment.

"I'm sorry. Everything went all funny there for a while. You were talking about poisoning and the flare gun, and suddenly I just got this awful desire to laugh."

"You were hysterical. That's what happened," Christabel told her. "I'm surprised we aren't all nuts by now."

Melanie grabbed Christabel by the sleeve. "When do the Holmbergs get here, Chris? How much longer till they come?"

"They'll get here this afternoon," she said. She glanced over at James for confirmation. "This afternoon? Isn't that what we figured?"

"Right." James nodded. "So we're all going to have to hang tough until then."

"Maybe you'll feel better after you eat something," Christabel told Melanie. "It's not much of a breakfast, but you ought to try to get something down."

She picked Melanie's mug of tea off the little end table.

"Here," she said, holding it up to Melanie's lips. "Drink this. Drink your tea."

Melanie took the cup from Christabel's hands, made a wry face, and said, "Yes, Mother."

She put the mug to her lips and took several long swallows. Then she stopped drinking, and a look of surprise came over her face, as though she couldn't figure out what was happening to her. She began to choke, dropping the mug and putting her hands to her throat. The mug fell to the floor. Tea puddled out around it.

We watched—stunned, helpless, just as we had when Tracy died.

Melanie's face seemed suffused with blood. Her lips twisted and turned blue. Her eyes stared angrily, accusingly, at us. Then she fell from the chair.

Christabel remained where she was, kneeling by the armchair. She seemed frozen in place.

I went to Melanie. Her eyes were still open, and she was twitching slightly. But then the twitching ceased.

James was at my side. He picked up Melanie's hand and felt her wrist.

Christabel stirred. "Are you . . . are you going to give her mouth-to-mouth or something?"

"It's too late," I said. "She's been poisoned."

James took Melanie's shirttail and wiped her lips carefully before attempting to give her artificial respiration.

We all knew it wouldn't do any good.

Melanie was dead.

SIXTEEN

James rose slowly, holding on to a chair for support. He wiped his hands on his jeans, the way he had before. With Tracy.

"Christabel," he said. "Why did you do it? Why'd you kill Melanie?"

I looked up at Christabel from my kneeling position. What I saw in her eyes made me come quickly to my feet and back away.

There was madness in her eyes.

The old Christabel—the Christabel I had known—had slipped away from behind her eyes. And now, swimming in those blue depths, was someone, or something, else. Something dark and deranged.

I moved closer to James.

"Yes, Christabel, why?" I asked. "First Chip.

Then Tracy and Ron. And now Melanie, your best friend. Why did you kill Melanie, Chris?"

She stood there, breathing heavily like an animal at bay. She glared wild-eyed first at James and then at me.

"It's been a conspiracy all along, hasn't it?" she shrilled. "The two of you against me. And now you're plotting to kill me!"

She spun around quickly and ran into the boys' bedroom. Before James and I could pull ourselves together and pursue her, she emerged triumphantly, holding something aloft.

"The flare gun," she told us with a great deal of satisfaction in her voice. "Thank you for telling me where it was, James."

"It isn't loaded, Chris," I said. "It's harmless now, you know."

She fumbled through the patch pockets of the jacket she was wearing and pulled out a flare.

"It was in the box in the corner. Close to where I laid my sleeping bag." She smiled gloatingly. "So I reached in and got it out when everyone was asleep. Am I smart or what?"

I'd read somewhere that you should always humor the dangerously insane. That was what I had to do. I had to get that flare from her before she put it in the gun and shot one of us.

A shiver of fear ran down my spine as I remembered Ron's death. Being shot by a flare gun must be an agonizing way to die. The phosphorus burns a hole in the body before it kills. Lucky for Ron he'd been shot in the head. It had killed him instantly.

"Give me the flare, Christabel," I said, holding out my hand and trying to speak in a soothing voice. "You might hurt yourself with it."

She laughed. "Oh, come on, Angie. Do you really think I'm *that* dumb?"

"Listen to her, Chris," James urged. "You're sick. You don't know what you're doing. Give us the flare, and we'll take care of you until the Holmbergs come. Then we'll get you to a hospital."

"You'll take care of me, all right," she said. "Real good care. So good that I'll wind up out there in the shed with Chip and Tracy."

James took a step toward her.

She inserted the flare into the gun and held it out before her. "Don't come any closer," she warned.

"Watch out, James," I cautioned.

Still holding the gun, aimed at us, with both hands, she slowly edged toward the door.

"Stay where you are," she commanded. "Don't try to come after me or I'll shoot."

She backed through the door and closed it behind her with a slam. We could hear her footsteps going down the stairs of the porch.

James ran over to the door and shot the bolt.

"What should we do now, James?"

"The first thing I'm going to do is try to stop shaking," he said.

I could see his hands where they rested on the doorjamb. They were trembling uncontrollably.

"Why?" I asked. "Why'd she do it? And why, then, did she act so frightened of being poisoned?"

"I guess it was just a big act to fool us."

"But where'd she get the cyanide, James? It *was* cyanide, wasn't it? Melanie's symptoms were the same as Tracy's."

"Uh-huh, I'm sure it was cyanide. She must have had the bottle tucked away somewhere. I don't know. We searched her belongings pretty carefully."

I went over to the door and pressed my ear to it.

"I can't hear her out there," I said. "If she fired the flare, could it come through the door?"

"No, we're safe enough if we stay here. She's probably gone into the woods. The woods overlooking the beach. She'll probably want to keep close to the water. Angie—what are you doing?"

I'd slid the bolt back and was opening the door a crack. I peered out cautiously.

"It's okay, James. I can't see her. You're right. She must have gone into the woods. She's probably watching the beach, although she seemed scared to death of Ron's body."

"That might have been an act, too."

"So what about when the Holmbergs arrive?" I asked. "What will she do? Try to kill them?"

"I've been thinking about that," James admitted worriedly. "Yeah, she probably will. Unless she's dreamed up one heck of a story to tell them, which I doubt."

"She only has one flare, though," I said. "She can't shoot both of them."

"She only needs to shoot Mr. Holmberg. Christabel can easily overpower his wife." James paused. "It's strange, though . . ."

"What?"

"Well, Christabel seemed so out of it,

mentally, right after Melanie died. But killing Tracy with the nasal spray and switching tea mugs with Melanie shows a lot more cunning than I would expect from someone like her."

"It's the why of it I don't understand," I said. "She's been acting so *normal*, yet obviously she's been insane all along. She *must* be out of her mind to kill her friends. But who would have guessed?"

"When I was recovering from my depression," James said, "I did a lot of reading about mental problems. A person can be a psychopath —totally remorseless and without conscience— and still be charming and likable and popular. Someone like that can really fool people."

"Is that what Christabel is? A psychopath?"

"Maybe. Or something close to it."

"And so, in the meantime," I said, "she's running around out there in the woods armed with a flare gun. And now she might attack the Holmbergs. Things seem to be getting worse and worse. I feel so helpless."

He put his arms around me. "We're going to get through this thing somehow. I promise you that."

I looked over to where Melanie lay beside her chair. She was flat on her back, the way

James had left her after trying to give her artificial respiration.

"What are we going to do about the . . . the body?" I asked. "We can't just leave her . . . it . . . here on the floor. But I really don't think I can bear to go into that shed again, James."

"No. Neither can I. Do you think you could help me get her into my bedroom? Would it bother you to touch her? We can lay her on one of the bunks."

Melanie wasn't at all heavy. I found myself wondering, as we carried her into the boys' room, if dead people weigh less than they do when alive. How much does the life force weigh?

I brought myself up sharply. Stop it, I thought. Pull yourself together, or you're going to become as hysterical as Melanie was just before she drank her poisoned tea.

We pulled a blanket over her and left the room silently, closing the door gently behind us. We had become quite expert on putting away dead bodies, I reflected. Maybe, when this was over, I should consider becoming a mortician. A bubble of laughter rose in my throat, but I choked it back.

"How'd Christabel do it?" I asked. "Do you

think it was when she said I'd given her the wrong cup?"

"It must have been. She must have pulled a shell game—you know, like they do at carnivals where they fool you about which shell covers the pea."

"And then she made sure Melanie drank her tea, remember?" I asked. "She actually held it up to Melanie's lips."

"Yeah. At the time I thought she was just being nice to Melanie." James shuddered. "Some friend!"

I'd put the bolt on the door again. At first we simply sat and stared at the fire. Then James began to pace restlessly. Up and down. Up and down. The cabin was so small. He brushed past me at every turn. I thought I would go mad.

"Stop it, James!" I finally snapped. Then I softened. "I'm sorry. It's my nerves. I'm afraid I'm going to lose it any minute now."

James dropped into a chair and ran his hands through his thick brown hair.

"I don't blame you, Angie. I feel that way, too."

He rubbed his face wearily. "I've been trying to figure out what to do. We can't just sit here all morning, waiting for the Holmbergs to come and rescue us. Christabel won't let them. She'll probably shoot Mr. Holmberg before he can even step out of the canoe."

"Is there any way we can warn them?"

"No. Not unless I stay down there on the beach, but then I'd be a sitting duck for Christabel."

"But she only has one flare," I said. "How does she think she's going to kill all of us with only one flare?"

"Who knows? Maybe she has some other weapon. She's done all right so far."

"So what should we do, then?"

"I'm going to go out and look for her," he said. "You know what they say. A good offense is the best defense."

I grabbed him by his arm. "No, James. She'll kill you."

"I can't just sit here and let the Holmbergs come paddling in to their deaths."

"That's very noble," I said coldly, "but stupid. After she kills you, she'll come for me. And then, with me out of the way, she'll have plenty of time to lure the Holmbergs to their doom. She's probably had this whole thing figured out in advance. She plans to commit the perfect crime. Crimes."

James freed himself from my grasp. Then he stood up, dragging me to my feet, too. He put his arms around me and held me to him so tightly, I could hear the beating of his heart.

"I'm going to find Christabel," he said. "I'm going to circle the woods that overlook the beach. She has to be there."

I started to protest, but he pressed my head against his shoulder.

"I'm not dumb, Angie. I can sneak up on her."

I lifted my head and looked up at him. "And then what?"

He smiled faintly. "I'm bigger and stronger than she is. If I take her by surprise, I know I can get the flare gun from her. And then, Angie, I'm going to do a very ungentlemanly thing. I'm going to knock her out cold."

SEVENTEEN

James was gone a long time. I figured he'd look under every rock and behind every tree for Christabel.

I heard his footsteps on the porch. They were heavy and slow.

I shot back the bolt and opened the door.

He looked tired. His face was pale and streaked with dirt, and his eyes were dark and sober.

"I couldn't find her, Angie," he said. "Not a trace."

"You looked in the woods by the beach?"

"Yeah. I must have tiptoed over every square inch of them."

"So where do you think she went?"

"She must have doubled back. She's got to be

on the island somewhere. There's no way off without a canoe."

I shivered. "You don't think she's hanging around the cabin, do you? I mean, out there, behind a tree or something?"

"I don't think so. She's probably off on the other side of the island, hiding out in the woods."

He scratched his head in puzzlement. "I don't know why she went that way, though."

"Maybe she doesn't know *what* she's doing anymore," I said. "She was pretty wacked out when she left here."

James went over to the fire and warmed his hands briefly at the blaze. "Well, I'd better go out and find her."

"You're going out again?" I asked.

"You know I have to," he said.

"Then I'm going with you."

"No, Angie. Stay here. Lock the door."

"No," I said. "I'd rather be with you than alone here, listening for noises and worrying about you."

I grabbed up my hooded sweatshirt and pulled it over my head.

"I guess there's no point in arguing with you," James said.

"No, there isn't. Oh, wait a minute, James."

I ran over to the trestle table and picked up a small paring knife, one we'd been using to peel fruit.

"If you think that's going to count as a weapon, you're wrong," James told me. "It's probably dull, besides."

"I don't care," I said. "I'll feel better carrying it. Every little bit helps."

We set out in the opposite direction from the beach.

It was eerily quiet in the woods. I don't know what happened to the birds we'd heard that morning. They must have all gone back into hiding. Once or twice a squirrel darted out from a hiding place, making us leap back in fear, but otherwise the woods were as quiet as a tomb.

Quiet as a *tomb*? I fought another rising bubble of laughter. What was wrong with me? Would I wind up as crazy as Christabel, the queen of Oakbridge High?

I'd been following close behind James. When he stopped abruptly, I nearly collided with him.

He spoke to me in a whisper. "I'm afraid we're doing this all wrong, Angie."

"Doing what wrong?"

"Sticking so close together."

"Why not?" I whispered back. "Aren't we safer this way?"

"No. She has the flare gun, remember? If she shoots at me and misses, she still has a chance of hitting you."

"Oh, God!" I said.

"So let's keep a couple of yards distance between us," he said. "We should keep far enough apart so that if she fires at one of us, she won't hit the other."

"You're not cheering me up, James," I said.

"One more thing," he said. "Keep a lookout for places like big rocks or clumps of bushes where she might be hiding."

"What do you *think* I've been doing?" I asked.

We moved on through the woods. James set the pace. Every now and then he'd hold up his hand and scout out a large rock or he'd peer behind a close-set stand of trees.

Very little sun managed to squeeze down through the trees and shine on us. It was so dark, it seemed like late afternoon, although it was still only midmorning.

Darkness, I thought. Always darkness. No wonder they named this place Shadow Island. Darkness and shadows and death. When this is over, I promised myself, I'm going to lie out in the sun every chance I get. Even if it turns my skin to alligator hide.

I knew James had spotted something when he stiffened up, just like a bird dog, and took a quick step backward.

I clutched my little paring knife tighter and ran over to him. "What is it, James?"

He didn't answer me. He didn't need to. His face was white. He raised a hand, which trembled as if he had palsy, and pointed.

It was Christabel.

She was lying up against a tree, her head resting on the trunk, as if she were taking a short break. Her eyes were open and staring, and her jaw was rigidly agape, as though she'd tried to scream. Her face was a peculiar blueish color. The flare gun lay on the ground beside her.

"She's dead," I said. "Christabel's dead."

Christabel was dead.

Christabel, then, was not the murderer.

And now there were two.

Only two.

James and I.

EIGHTEEN

So this was it. This was how it was supposed to end. This was the way it had been planned right from the start. The two of us, killer and victim. Final victim.

For a brief moment we said nothing. We simply stared into each other's eyes. What were we looking for? A reprieve from death? An explanation? Forgiveness?

But what can a victim say to change a murderer's mind? What argument is strong enough to stop a killing machine?

And why should a murderer try to explain why it was necessary to kill five—soon to be six—people? For forgiveness?

Do you need forgiveness when you've committed the perfect crime, or is that only for those who will get caught?

This murderer would not get caught. . . .

NINETEEN

I sidestepped cautiously over to Christabel's body, keeping an eye on James and holding my pitiful little paring knife out between us.

Then I bent down quickly and picked up the flare gun.

"So this is it," I said softly, circling warily around James. "The end. Just the two of us."

He made no move to intercept me, to try to get the flare gun away from me. He just stared at me, dazed and unbelieving.

"Angie?" His voice was weak. I could barely hear him. "It was you? *You* killed all those people . . . our friends. I can't believe it!"

I stopped circling and smiled. It was a good feeling, that smile.

"Believe it. And I did it well, didn't I? You never suspected, did you?"

James was trembling. I could see it. I could see his whole body quiver. Even his lips trembled. I felt powerful, watching him tremble. Powerful and justified.

"But . . . but why?" he managed to gasp out.

He'd taken a step forward. I held out my knife and said, "Don't come any closer, James. If you do, I'll cut you with this, just like I did Christabel."

A look of bewilderment came over his face. "You killed Christabel with *that*?"

"It looks harmless, doesn't it?" I said, laughing, amused by his confusion. "But this isn't just an ordinary paring knife, James. It's been dipped in curare. You've heard of curare, haven't you? It's that poisonous stuff South American Indians use on their arrows. The smallest cut kills instantly."

James shook his head. "Curare? What are you talking about? How'd you ever get your hands on something like that?"

"If you want to murder someone," I told him, "it really comes in handy to have a daddy who owns a string of pharmacies. I bet you didn't know they used this stuff in medicine, did you, James? It isn't fatal when taken orally. Only when it reaches the bloodstream through a cut or puncture."

James seemed to be pulling himself together. I saw him take several deep breaths, as if to calm himself. His shaking ceased. He was looking at me now with clear eyes. He'd even put his hand in his pocket, a rather casual stance, I thought, considering what was about to happen to him. Considering he was about to die.

"I'm sorry, James. I didn't mean to ramble on."

He looked at me steadily for a few seconds before he asked, "So what happens now, Angie?"

"You mean, you haven't guessed?"

"I'm your next victim, right?"

I nodded.

"I never thought it was you," he said. "I was sure it was one of the others. I thought you were too honest and straight and . . . wonderful."

He smiled that wry little smile of his. The smile that had almost—*almost*—made me weaken and fall in love with him.

"I thought you were really special, Angie,"

he said sadly, shaking his head. "Really special."

"We had a lot going for us," I agreed. "We would have made a great couple. It's too bad circumstances made any kind of a relationship between us impossible."

"What circumstances? What on earth would make you want to kill your friends?"

"Are you trying to stall for time, James? Or do you have some crazy idea you can get me talking and then jump me and take away my knife?"

I raised the flare gun and pointed it directly at him. My hand didn't tremble. Not the least little bit. I was proud of my steady nerves.

"I have two weapons, you know," I told him. "And I think you know how painful it would be if I shot you with this flare gun. So don't try anything stupid, James. Behave yourself and I'll give you a quick death with the curare."

"I won't try to jump you, Angie. But if you're going to kill me, I'd like to know why. You owe me that much."

I took a tighter grip on the flare gun. I had no intention of using it on him, but I didn't want him to know that. I liked James in spite of, well, everything. I wouldn't want his death to be a painful one.

"All right, then," I said. "Fair enough. I'll tell you why. I'm going to kill you because you were there at the murder and you did nothing to stop it."

"Whose murder? Chip's? Tracy's? Ron's?"

"No, not those," I said. "Besides, they were executions, not murders. Legal executions, although the case never came to court. Except for Tracy, though. She was just an innocent bystander."

"I don't understand," he said. "I haven't the slightest idea what you're talking about."

"I think you do," I told him evenly.

James *is* stalling for time, I thought. Just like in a murder mystery where the victim keeps the murderer talking so he can survive until the police come. Well, James could do his best, but it wouldn't keep him from being executed. The Holmbergs weren't due for at least three hours. Plenty of time to explain everything and then do what needed to be done.

Besides, I wanted to tell James everything. I needed to tell him. The others were fools. James was different. He was like me. I wanted to tell him what I had done, and how I'd done it. I wanted to see the admiration in his eyes before I killed him. I needed it to justify what I was doing.

"I was present at a murder, you said. What murder?"

His voice was patient and soothing. Too soothing. Humoring, even. Like I had gone around the bend and he had to settle me down. So he thought I was insane, did he? I was saner and more practical than he'd ever be.

"What murder?" he repeated.

"The murder of Michael Giddings," I said.

James drew in his breath and took a step backward. Now who needed soothing?

"But . . . but that wasn't murder," he protested weakly.

"Yes, it was," I said. "Unfortunately, however, no court in the land would see it as that. But it was murder all the same. You took advantage of Michael's innocence. You five—Ron, Christabel, Melanie, Chip, and you—deliberately got Michael drunk at a stupid party and then put him in his car and let him drive home. Except that he never reached home, did he? He drove off a cliff and was burned to death when the car exploded."

I held back my tears. I couldn't let myself

cry. Not yet, anyway. Those tears would come in handy later, when I told the Holmbergs how I'd had to fight James for my life. How I couldn't believe he was the murderer—I was in love with him, of course—until we found Chris, and then he'd gone crazy and tried to kill me, too.

"What happened to Michael Giddings was an accident, Angie," James said. "It was terrible and pointless, but it was an accident, not murder. And why was he so important to you that you'd commit murder for him?"

"I loved Michael more than anything in the world," I told him. "I don't think you could possibly understand how I felt about him."

James opened his mouth to say something—something disbelieving, judging from the expression on his face—but I cut him off.

"Yes, yes I know," I said. "I was only sixteen, and sixteen-year-old girls get crushes. But this wasn't just a silly crush, James. Every now and then two people are selected by . . . fate, I guess you can call it, to be partners. Perfect partners. And that's what Michael and I were."

"Then what was he doing at that party?" James asked. His voice was cruel and cutting.

"Christabel's party? He came by himself, not with you."

I could feel my face turn red.

"Michael," I said, "had a philosopher's love of beauty. And Christabel is . . . was . . . beautiful. It was only a temporary infatuation. He would have seen right through her. Maybe he had, before the party ended."

I couldn't hold the tears back now. They were running down my cheeks.

"He wangled an invitation to that party. I told him not to go. I said they weren't his kind of people. I'd heard Christabel laughing at him behind his back, calling him a 'geek.' I hated her for that. A geek? Michael? Why, she wasn't even worthy to tie his shoes. He had a brilliant mind and dreams of using it to change the world for the better."

James held out his hand. "Please, Angie—"

"And you, you miserable pack of hyenas, you thought it would be a big joke to get 'the geek' drunk. Well, you succeeded, didn't you? And then you put him in his car. Why didn't you just put a bullet through his brain? It would have been a more merciful death than being burned alive."

"I had nothing to do with it, Angie," James

said. His face was ashen. "I'd been drinking that night, too. That's why I've quit. And that's why I had that nervous breakdown. The thought of what happened that night made me sick. Physically and mentally sick."

"No, you didn't feed him the liquor, but you stood by and watched, didn't you?" I accused. "And you didn't say anything. You're the worst kind of murderer, James. The kind that just stands there and does nothing. That's why I saved you for last. For the poetic justice of it. So you could stand by—again—and do nothing."

"I see," James said quietly. "So when did you decide to . . . avenge Michael?"

I wiped the tears from my cheeks with the back of the hand that held the flare gun.

"Immediately," I replied. "I knew I'd have to be accepted by Christabel and the rest of your stupid group first, though. That's when I lost weight, got a new wardrobe and hairstyle, and ditched my glasses for contact lenses. People started treating me differently right away. What fools!"

"I always liked you, Angie," James said softly, "even when you wore those funny horn-rims." But I wasn't paying any attention to his words now.

"I only did it for Michael," I said. "I never felt personal beauty was all that important. But it certainly opened the right doors at Oakbridge High. My new good looks brought me instant 'popularity' and an entrée into your elite 'in' group—that simpering group of sadistic morons. But I went along with all of you. I had my plan, and I had to go at it step by step."

"This trip, then. You'd planned for that?"

"Not really. But I knew that sooner or later the right opportunity would present itself. The trip was a gift from heaven. I made sure I got myself included. Then I had to think of some way to get rid of our faithful chaperons, the Holmbergs."

"Did you have something to do with their getting sick?"

I laughed. "Cocoa made with a strong chocolate-flavored laxative is quite delicious, James, but a bit too rich for most of us."

"But the canoes—"

"I was the one who shoved them into the water that first night. I knew the winds would be coming from a northwest direction—I'd listened to the weather report—and that they would blow the canoes across the lake. I wanted

208

us to be isolated. I knew I didn't have much time to accomplish everything I had planned."

"And so you killed Chip the first evening."

"He was easy," I boasted. "What guy ever thinks he's going to get bashed in the head by a pretty girl? Chip was always a fool."

"But what about Tracy?" James asked. "You liked Tracy. You cried when she died. Were you faking then, too?"

"No." I shook my head soberly. "I didn't want to kill Tracy, but I had to. She hadn't been responsible for Michael's death, but she *would* insist on coming on this trip—so, in a way, it was her own fault."

"How'd you do it, Angie?"

"I knew the kind of nasal spray she used. Didn't we all? So it was no problem to substitute it for one loaded with a nice dose of cyanide. I'm a science nerd, remember? And my father owns a bunch of pharmacies. I can go into those places anytime I want. Poor Tracy. Well, at least she doesn't have to worry about her allergies anymore."

James looked shocked. "You're crazy, Angie!"

I looked at him through narrowed eyes. "Not crazy. I just believe in justice, James. An eye for an eye, and a tooth for a tooth. I didn't want to kill Tracy, but what else could I do? In every war there are innocent casualties."

"And Ron. Was he an innocent casualty?"

"Are you kidding? He was the worst of the bunch. He was the one who made sure Michael drank too much. I wanted him to suffer when he died. That's why I used the flare. But then I had to shoot him in the head so he wouldn't scream and give me away."

"And then you killed Melanie," James continued. "Where'd you store the cyanide? We looked through everyone's gear."

"I had it in a tiny bottle, and put it in my flashlight, after I'd taken the batteries out. That's where the curare was, too. Remember how I told you my flashlight was broken, and you gallantly shared yours with me?"

"I remember a lot of things, Angie."

"Christabel unwittingly helped me kill Melanie. She made all that fuss about getting the right cup. So while she was carrying on, I substituted mine, which I'd put the cyanide into when no one was looking. I hope old Melanie's life flashed before her eyes before she died."

"You really hated Melanie, didn't you?" James asked.

"I sure did. Now, there was one murder I enjoyed committing."

"Did you also enjoy killing Christabel?"

"I was too busy with that one to enjoy it. I had to hurry off when you were down at the beach to do the job. I'd seen her go off in the opposite direction when I peeked out after she'd left. Remember that? I told you I couldn't see her, but I lied."

"I never guessed, Angie. You're quite an actress. Maybe you should consider the stage rather than a science laboratory for your future."

I acknowledged that with a grimace and continued. "I knew you'd spend some time in the woods overlooking the beach, so I dashed off in the direction I'd seen her take. She was so gullible, James. I acted scared to death. I told her I'd found out for sure that you were the killer, and she got downright hysterical with relief when I promised her she and I were going to knock you off. So when she wasn't looking, I hit her with the curare-dipped paring knife. It was all too simple, really."

I'd been so intent on my story that I hadn't noticed that James had been quietly closing the gap between us.

"Get back!" I commanded. "Don't try to do anything smart, James, or I swear I'll shoot you with this flare."

He raised both hands placatingly and backed away.

"So what happens now?" he asked. "You'll kill me, of course. Mercifully, with the curare, if I behave myself. But what are you going to tell the Holmbergs when they arrive?"

"Why, I'll be in shock, James. I'll be pale and disheveled, but still beautiful. The lovely, innocent schoolgirl who has miraculously survived death. Your body will be there, beside Christabel's. You killed her with the poisoned knife and tried to use it on me. We struggled, and you got cut. It was self-defense, pure and simple. I'll even rip my shirt and bruise myself with a rock to make it look realistic."

James thought my story over for a moment and then said, "Very good, Angie. It seems like you've thought of just about everything. But what about my motive for murder? Why would I kill my friends?"

"Elementary, my dear James. You've had a nervous breakdown, remember? Through my tears I will manage to tell the Holmbergs how strange you'd been acting. And then how, when

212

Chip was killed, we all suspected you but weren't sure. But when Tracy died and then Ron . . . well, rest assured, I will do a superb job of convincing them that you went off your rocker and did in all the happy campers. Except me, of course. Beautiful, brave me. It will be my finest hour, James. What a shame you won't be here to see."

"Maybe I will," he said.

James seemed to be listening to something. He narrowed his eyes and squinted at something over my shoulder.

"I hope you aren't trying to make me turn around and look at something, James," I said. "Please don't insult my intelligence with an old trick like that!"

"It appears your hot-laxative cocoa wasn't as potent as you thought," he said. Then he raised his voice and shouted, "Over here! We're over here!"

I edged around behind him, still holding the gun on him, and looked in the direction he was shouting.

From where we were, we could just barely see the cabin through the woods.

James wasn't faking.

The Holmbergs were wearily climbing up

the front steps. They must have left before dawn, the damned eager beavers!

"Over here!" James yelled again. "Hurry!"

I saw the Holmbergs stop and look our way.

It was hard to see them clearly at that distance and through the trees, but they were coming toward us, that was for sure.

It was too late to kill James. What would I do now?

"There's no such thing as a perfect crime, Angie," James said.

"Oh yeah?" I sneered.

Thinking quickly, I wiped my prints from the gun and the knife with my shirttail and threw them to the ground. Then I began tearing my shirt.

"Now it will be your word against mine, James," I said. "But *you're* the one who's had the nervous breakdown. I have a feeling *I'm* the one they'll believe. They came in the nick of time and saved my life. Your hollering at them was just another ruse—another sign of your nutty behavior. That's what I'll make them think, anyway."

James bent over and picked up the knife and the flare gun.

I stopped tearing at my shirt and stared at him, astonished by his stupidity.

"Thank you, James. Now *your* fingerprints will be on the weapons. I thought you were supposed to be smart."

"But I am, Angie," James replied calmly. "I just wanted to make sure you don't change your mind and let me have it with either of these things. I have no desire that my life end the way my friends' did."

"But your fingerprints, dummy!"

"They don't matter," James says. "What really matters is this."

He reached into his pocket and pulled out something.

It was his miniature tape recorder.

He held it up so I could see. The wheels were still turning. Still taping.

"I put it in my pocket when I went out after Christabel," he explained. "I wanted to tape what she said so that, in case something happened to me, no one could blame you for the murders."

I couldn't speak.

"But now I've taped everything *you* said," James told me. "Everything you said is right here. I guess you forgot I was an audio freak."

I had to clear my throat before I could get my voice under control.

"Yes, you're an audio freak and I'm a science nerd. The freaks," I said with rising hysteria, "have triumphed over the nerds."

Hot tears were streaming down my cheeks as the Holmbergs came toward us, calling our names.

Don't miss this terrifying thriller
by
Kate Daniel

Sweetheart

The flashing blue and red lights were beautiful. As she focused her camera, Jessie McAllister tried not to think about what they meant. The blue was the purest of ice-blues, the red a brilliant crimson. In the fading twilight, the blood on the pavement looked like a pool of oil, all color drained from it by the lights rotating on top of the squad car.

Jessie snapped the shutter, then moved around the end of the car for a closer look. She had been on her way home when she'd passed the scene of the accident. She'd reached for her camera out of instinct. Since she'd gotten her first Instamatic for her eighth birthday, she'd taken pictures of everything. The old Mamiya she carried now had been given to her for Christmas her junior year of high school, and she always carried it. But she'd never taken pictures of a fatal accident before. She didn't know what had happened; there were no wrecked cars nearby, but a still form lay in the gutter. A backpack on the ground nearby spilled out books. Jessie took a picture of the bag, wondering if the victim had been a student at the university.

Jessie took another shot, multiple shadows caused by all the different lights. As a photography major at the University of Arizona, she was learning that good pictures could turn up anyplace, and some of them would be ugly. Jessie noticed she wasn't the only one here with a camera. A police photographer was moving around, getting shots of the scene from several angles. His flash unit lit up the body of the young woman briefly, and Jessie looked away. She couldn't bring herself to take pictures of something that gruesome.

The normally busy street was blocked off. People swarmed around the victim, busy with the aftermath of tragedy. Several police-squad cars lined the road, all with flashers going, as well as a van marked Tucson Police Department. An ambulance stood nearby, but the three paramedics beside it weren't doing anything. It was too late for this victim. Yellow plastic tape had been strung around a section of the street, with the words POLICE/FIRE LINE—DO NOT CROSS stamped in black letters along the length of it. Inside the tape, a tired-looking man in a gray suit looked down at the body, while another paramedic knelt beside it. Behind the man in the suit, a uniformed officer laughed at something someone had said. Jessie focused on their contrasting expressions and clicked the shutter again. The tired man looked up at the flash, and his eyes met Jessie's briefly, then he bent over to speak with the paramedic. Tire marks—streaks of burned rubber—led away from the body, swerving from the curb, then continuing for a few feet. The police tape paralleled them. Jessie got a shot of the black lines and curb framed by the tape. As she did, the police photographer knelt down beside her and took a picture of the marks as well.

Behind her, she could hear a woman's voice. ". . . just came right *at* her!" The voice dissolved into sobs. Jessie turned. A couple dressed in jogging suits stood just outside the taped area, speaking to a woman dressed in slacks and a warm-looking windbreaker. The jogger was crying, her partner's arm around her. As they spoke, the other woman made notes. The trio didn't look around when Jessie's flash went off. Twilight had faded from the sky and she shivered, realizing how cold it had become. Even in Arizona, January nights are cold, and the sharp wind was cutting through Jessie's University of Arizona sweatshirt.

Jessie turned away from the joggers to retrieve her bike, which she'd parked by a tree, then stopped again. Paramedics were wheeling a stretcher toward the body. She raised her camera to take one final picture of the end of the drama, then she froze. Through her telephoto lens, she could see the face of the victim. And it looked familiar.

Jessie stared. With fumbling hands, she automatically snapped the lens cap back on her camera and zipped it into its case. Jessie moved along the tape until she was directly opposite the body, and for the first time, looked at the sightless eyes. Her throat suddenly dry, Jessie ducked under the tape. It was Laurie.

Before she could get any closer, a hand grasped her upper arm. "Back behind the tape, miss," said a firm voice. The woman who'd been questioning the witnesses stepped in front of her and continued, "It's there for a reason. Now if you'll just move back. . . ." The woman broke off as Jessie continued to stare at Laurie. The crew from the ambulance spread a blanket over the body, cutting off the nightmarish sight of that dead gaze. Jessie shuddered.

The woman's official tone of voice shifted slightly. "Do you recognize her?" At Jessie's faint nod, she said, "I think we'd better ask you some questions." She raised her voice slightly. "Ramon?"

The man in the gray suit broke away from the group around the corpse and joined them. "What you got, Mary?" There was a flash of recognition in his face as he frowned at Jessie's camera case. "Newspaper?"

"No." Jessie swallowed hard. "Is that—I think that's Laurie Birkson. Is it?"

"That's what the ID says," he said. "Did you know her?" He motioned to one of the uniformed police officers standing nearby, and spoke with him in a low voice. Jessie couldn't keep her eyes off the small group around the body. Around *Laurie*. The body, now wrapped in a blanket, was being carefully slipped into a large bag. *Body bag*, Jessie thought. *That's what they call those things. Laurie is in a body bag.*

"You all right, miss?" The officer's hand was under her elbow as Jessie turned away from the grim scene. Jessie realized she was dizzy. She nodded—a tiny gesture that moved her head less than an inch—and found her voice again.

"I'm fine." Her voice shook as she spoke.

"I'm Detective Gutierrez," the man said, "and this is Detective Peters. Would you take a look at this, please?" He held out an open wallet, and Jessie glanced down at it. An Arizona driver's license was in the plastic holder.

"Yes, that's her." This time her voice almost sounded normal. "Laurie Birkson. She's in my English class."

"You a student? Your name, please?" the detective asked.

Jessie noticed that he was jotting down her answers in a small notebook. She gave her name and address, and added, "We're both freshmen. I think Laurie's from Yuma. I don't know her that well. She works at the library." The words rang in her ears as Jessie realized they were wrong. Laurie *had* worked at the library. She wouldn't any longer. And Jessie would never get to know her well.

He grunted, a noncommittal sound. "That matches the license. Did you see it happen?"

Jessie shook her head. "I'm not even sure what happened. Hit and run?" He grunted again, and she went on, "I was riding home—I work at Sweeny's."

"Riding?" She pointed at her bike on the sidewalk. It had fallen on its side.

"When did you recognize her?" The question was abrupt, and Jessie realized the police must have been here for some time, asking questions of everyone who'd witnessed the hit and run. He probably wondered why she hadn't said anything sooner. She explained, emphasizing that she hadn't been focusing on the body in her pictures. It was only when she had gotten a clear-enough look at the face that she'd realized who it was. Jessie swallowed hard. She didn't like to remember that terror-filled face, or those vacant eyes.

He seemed to accept her explanation. Glancing at her camera again, he changed the subject. "What were you taking all the pictures for?"

"I'm majoring in photography," she answered. "And Mr. Sweeny—I told you I work at Sweeny's Studio—Mr. Sweeny keeps telling me I should always have my camera ready." She broke off. "I wasn't taking pictures of—of Laurie, I told you that. Just the people, and the lights, and the ambulance, and everything." She waved her hand, indicating all the activity around them.

"Yeah." Detective Gutierrez nodded and shut the notebook. Behind him, the stretcher with the bag containing Laurie was being wheeled into an unmarked minibus. Ambulances were for the living. "All right. Thanks for your cooperation, but next time you see a police tape, stay behind it. See Miss McAllister back to her bicycle, Mary." He smiled slightly. "Ride carefully, miss." The smile faded as he turned away. Detective Peters nodded and led Jessie back to the edge of the taped-off area.

Jessie felt sick. She'd seen dead animals alongside the road, and once she'd seen a car hit a dog. She'd been to a few funerals, where the dead person was made up to look like they were asleep. But she'd never seen anything like this. Laurie's face had been untouched, but the rest of her—death had left Laurie crumpled and bloody. This wasn't like a funeral, where the body looked as artificial as a store mannequin. It was real.

By the time she reached her apartment building five blocks away, Jessie was shaking all over. She managed to fasten the chain lock on her bike, then she headed for her apartment. Before she reached the door, it was pulled open from inside by her roommate, Valerie King.

"Jessie, where've you been?" her roommate asked. "The show starts in forty-five minutes!" Light spilled out of the apartment around Val, making a halo of her short blond hair. She was already dressed, Jessie noted with a pang, wearing the lapis-blue sweater she'd bought the week before, and her matching blue dangle earrings. Val looked great, and she knew it. Jessie had forgotten all about the double date they had planned for the evening. She felt grubby; she wanted to take a shower. There wasn't any blood on her, but she felt as though she were covered in it.

The guys were already there. The two huge football players seemed to fill the entire apartment. Val's date, Art Ducas, straddled a kitchen chair. Randy Beckman, Jessie's boyfriend, came and greeted her with a hug. As they walked into the living room, he put his arm around her waist.

"Something's the matter," Randy stated. "What happened?" He sank onto the couch, pulling her with him, his arm tightening around her slightly.

"I'm late," Jessie said.

Art crossed his arms on the back of the chair and looked at her. Val's boyfriend was so big that the ordinary kitchen chair looked like it had come from a dollhouse. "No joke. What kept you?"

Jessie could still see the expression on Laurie's face as she said, "There was an accident over on Fourth Avenue, just down from the studio. Hit and run. I didn't see it happen, but I got there while the cops were asking people questions, and I—I recognized who it was. It was Laurie Birkson. She's dead."

"Dead!" The exclamation burst from Val.

"I told them I knew her, and they asked me about a million questions." Jessie stopped as she gave way to the shakes once more.

"Easy," Randy said. His large hands moved with surprising delicacy as he stroked Jessie's dark hair. "Anybody'd be shook up, seeing someone they know like that. Do the cops have any idea who did it?"

Jessie shook her head, not trying to speak.

"I know her—*knew* her—enough to say hi, but that's about all," Val said. "Mostly from the library. Didn't you say she was in your English class, Jessie?"

"She *was* in my English class," Jessie said, "and she was a photography major, too. She was in my Art Survey course last semester, and I've seen her around the Center."

"You want to just forget about going out tonight?" Randy asked, still stroking her hair.

"I don't even want to move off this couch," Jessie said.

"I don't blame you," Val said. "We can see the movie some other time."

"I didn't know her," Art remarked. "But if you don't want to go out, that's cool."

Val turned to him. "You must have known her, Art. The redhead who worked on the main desk at the library? Brenda's friend?"

He shook his head. "She may have known your ex-roommate, but that doesn't mean I knew her," he said. "There's a lot of people who work at the library. Who knows who they are?"

The University of Arizona was a big school, with a total enrollment larger than the population of Jessie's hometown, Bisbee. Laurie had been majoring in the same subject as Jessie, yet they'd only shared a couple of classes, and had hardly known each other. They liked some of the same photographers and had shared English assignments. That was about it. Art was right; there were way too many people on campus to know them all.

"All right, so you don't want to go out," Art said. "But let's do something, not just talk about her."

Val made popcorn, and they put a video on, but Jessie couldn't shake the memory. The guys left early, and she went to bed. With luck, she wouldn't have nightmares about Laurie.

Jessie went directly to Sweeny's Studio the next morning. She had only two classes on Fridays, but she was cutting them to go with her boss on a shoot. Jack Sweeny had been hired to take pictures at the Desert Museum for a new fund-raising campaign, and he was taking Jessie along as his assistant. He was an old friend of her father's, which was how she'd gotten the job at the studio. Jobs at a good studio such as Sweeny's were always at a premium, and freshmen didn't normally get a chance at them.

Jessie got to Sweeny's an hour early, since she wanted to develop the pictures she'd taken the night before. Like many studios, Sweeny's sent color film out to be developed, but they also had a darkroom for processing black and white work. By the time Jack was ready to leave for the museum, the pictures were finished. Jessie took the prints along, intending to show them to Jack later.

Jack flipped on the radio as soon as they got into the jeep. Jessie hated the light-rock station, but it was Jack's jeep and he was the boss. As they headed west, Jack began telling her what they'd be doing and why jobs such as this were worth more than the amount they paid. He was fond of lecturing, and Jessie usually enjoyed it. But right now her mind was on the photos of Laurie, and she wasn't listening. As they passed the interstate, the music stopped and was followed by a newscast. Jessie leaned forward, listening closely to the report. After a few minutes there was a story about the hit and run. The reporter said that the police hadn't found the driver of the murder vehicle.

Murder? The newscast continued, saying witnesses—Jessie thought of the joggers—had told police the car had deliberately headed for the victim. The car, which had been reported stolen, had been found a half-mile away, the keys still in the ignition.

Jessie stared ahead, seeing nothing of the mountains in front of her. Murder was a word on the news or a TV cop show. It wasn't a word to use about people, real people, people she knew. The joggers must have been mistaken. The sudden silence as the radio was turned off broke Jessie's daze, and she realized Jack had spoken to her a couple of times.

"Sorry, Mr. Sweeny." She looked over at him. "What'd you say?"

"What I was saying before can wait," he said. "That story hit you pretty hard. Someone you knew?"

Jessie nodded. "Yeah, but that's not all. I *saw* it." As they started the steep climb up to Gates Pass, she told him about the shock of seeing a dead body, the double shock of realizing she knew the person, and taking pictures of the whole thing.

"And that was why you were in early, huh?" He slowed for the first of the sharp bends as the road twisted up the canyon. "Get any good shots?"

Jessie's hand groped automatically for the handle on the dash as she leaned against the curve. "I think so. I've got them with me; I was planning to ask you to look at them later."

"I don't want to right now, that's for sure." He downshifted as they climbed again, stuck behind a motor home with out-of-state plates.

"Let's hope that snowbird doesn't roll off a cliff," Jack said, referring to the tourist. Such vehicles had no business on this road; it was too narrow and dangerous, but some people always tried it. They reached a short straight stretch, and with a sigh of relief Jack managed to pass the motor home. "Remind me to take a look at your pictures when we get done at the museum. Any shots of your friend, what was her name, Laura?" They slowed for the sharp bend that marked the top of the pass. It was a tight squeeze, with steep cliffs falling away on the other side.

"Laurie," Jessie corrected him. "No, I didn't recognize her at first, but I didn't want to take pictures of a corpse."

"Take the pictures. Always take the pictures. If you decide later you don't want them, fine, you can throw them out. But if you don't take them and then decide you want them, you're out of luck. That's one of the most important things you have to learn, Jessie." She had triggered one of his favorite lectures. She'd heard it a hundred times since she'd started work at the studio last fall. It was good advice, too, but this time Jessie didn't concentrate. Instead, as he spoke she pulled out the pictures and looked at them once more. Here were the tire marks, the stark shadows cast by the bright lights, the joggers arm in arm as the woman wept and Detective Peters quietly took notes.

A detail in one picture—the backpack spilling into the gutter—caught her eye, and she looked at it more closely. A small stuffed animal any student at the university would recognize was halfway out of the bag. It was the Wildcat, the mascot of the University of Arizona. But this one had on a miniature football jersey with the number 27 on it. Jessie had a similar one in her room, number 63. It was Randy's; the Wildcats team had been presented with these special Wildcat toys earlier in the month, at the end of a successful season. The Alumni Association had had them made up special. Each one had a player's number on it, and they'd made a big deal of presenting them at the banquet. They were supposed to be unique.

Jessie stared at the picture, puzzled. The night before, Art had said he didn't know Laurie. But 27 was Art's number.

Sweet Goodbyes

A wonderful series of heart-rending stories that will make you cry. Ordinary high-school girls are suddenly forced to cope with a life-threatening illness. Things will never be the same again, as each girl fights to survive...

Please Don't Go
Losing David
Life Without Alice
My Sister, My Sorrow
Goodbye, Best Friend
The Dying of the Light

All at £2.99

Order Form

To order direct from the publishers, just make a list of the titles you want and fill in the form below:

Name ....

Address ....

....

....

Send to: Dept 6, HarperCollins Publishers Ltd, Westerhill Road, Bishopbriggs, Glasgow G64 2QT.

Please enclose a cheque or postal order to the value of the cover price, plus:

UK & BFPO: Add £1.00 for the first book, and 25p per copy for each addition book ordered.

Overseas and Eire: Add £2.95 service charge. Books will be sent by surface mail but quotes for airmail despatch will be given on request.

A 24-hour telephone ordering service is avail-able to Visa and Access card holders: 041-772 2281